[*Enter Ghost*]

[*Enter Ghost*]

Tom Vander Ven

Illustrated by Cyndi Vander Ven
and artists from the Mixel 1.0 community

Wolfson Press
Indiana University South Bend

The author is grateful to the editors for finding a place
for some of these pieces in their publications:
Michigan Quarterly Review, *Indiana University Alumni
Magazine*, *Tri-City Times* [Imlay City, Michigan],
The Beloit Poetry Journal, *Poetry Daily* (online),
*Poetry Daily: 366 Poems from the World's Most Popular
Website* (print), *Confluence: The Journal of Graduate
Liberal Studies*, *Currents* [Indiana University South
Bend], and *Andover Bulletin*.

Cover design by Cyndi Vander Ven
Interior art by members of the Mixel 1.0 community
Design and editorial team:
Ken Smith and David James.

ISBN: 978-1-939674-01-2

Wolfson Press
Master of Liberal Studies Program
Indiana University South Bend
1700 Mishawaka Avenue
South Bend, Indiana 46634-7111
wolfson.iusb.edu

TABLE OF CONTENTS

Mixel 1.0 Illustrations

ACKNOWLEDGMENTS

All the talk about exile in this book! All the gauzy layers and shimmering spaces that separate us from ourselves and all that is the other! All the special effects thereof. Now, then, this sprawling Diamond Jubilee limited edition offering of poems, stories, essays, and plays! Just how many chances do we get in our daily, dulling lives to speak of the crepuscular and the numinous?

I herewith reaffirm and give thanks to that word, "sprawl," after sixty years under its cloud, having used it to describe an aunt and cousin asleep on our living room floor one morning before Christmas and having had withheld for a day as punishment my sugarplum gift—a glamorous yellow-and-brown, plastic, signature Arthur Godfrey ukelele. It came with a device that clamped over the frets so that I only had to hold down a button to change chords. My Eric Claptonesque career stalled beyond recovery.

Two years ago, Ken Smith and Joe Chaney proposed this book, some mélange of my writings, seen and unseen. They are major figures in IUSB's Department of English, the Master of Liberal Studies program, and the university's Wolfson Press. And I'm glad to have concluded my academic career after theirs began. Twelve years after my retirement, they remain my friends and colleagues. Joe Chaney's introduction to this book creates the persuasive illusion of a coherent motif, and I am grateful to him for his thoughtful reading. As the editor for two books and a short story, Ken has always been insightful, patient, and caring of manuscripts and their incarnations. A writer could not ask for more. The editorial work of Ken bears out what I wrote to him in 1994, soon after he began his career at IUSB: "Our conversation yesterday confirms my high hopes for your leadership of the writing program. The air seems very clear and mild around your brain, and I think your colleagues will enjoy your weather."

Countless figures to thank rise out of the graying mists of Michigan, Massachusetts, Wyoming, Colorado, Indiana, and Georgia. Too many to name without slighting others—family, friends, chancellors, colleagues, teachers, and students. Sailors, handball players, and tennis players. Actors, directors, stage managers, and costumers. "Eumaios, oh, my swineherd!" If your name doesn't appear somewhere in these pages, write it in. You belong here.

To all my family and ancestors, all the migrants of human history out of Africa, into Europe, from Germany to the Netherlands, and to Virginia and Michigan, thanks for the genes which together with the advances of medical science have gotten me to this jubilee. In that northerly, westerly arc, the ancestral saga, there was in my father's lineage a story of an avuncular Spanish Jew, whom I mention to add guitar to the Dutch migrant trudge.

I thank the models of learning in my family—our mother's college degrees in the 1920s and her high goals of education and determination for her four children. After my parents' divorce, she held the family together by teaching, thrift, and fretting. Like the faux-grandma in Bellow's *Augie March*, who told the boys again and again, "Just so you want," our mother insisted that we carry with us a great hunger for learning. Ned, the physicist, and Jack, the historian and librarian, and younger Mary, our Spanish language resource, formed a phalanx of study. And music! Always a piano in the house, and recordings of great works, symphonies and operas, and before school, "The J. L. Hudson Minute Parade" of classical music on a Detroit radio station. We made trips on the bus line to *Carmen* and to the Art Institute of Detroit for the Renaissance art exhibit. And every winter night, we banked the coal fire in the furnace and on the weekend dragged a tub of ashes to the curb. Did we pause to give thanks for central heating? Or for the bottles from Twin Pines Dairy that appeared in the milk chute by the side door? Or the diapered figure of a national spirit opposite Sibelius's "Finlandia" in *The Silver Book of Song*? The thanks are in the singing: "Glorious Apollo from on high beheld us wandering to find a temple for his praise. . . ."

And thanks to the children who have found their ways so well, whether because of us or in spite of us: Maria, a reading specialist and master elementary teacher; Tom, a highly accomplished professor and sociologist; Erika, whose missions work has taken her to Germany,

China, and Ireland; and Ashleigh, who, despite her illness, manages so bravely and well her career and studies. Thanks to the promising lives of our grandchildren, Tory, Sam, Luke, and Skylar, for whom we are small figures on the horizon. And Ashleigh's child, yet unborn.

There are so many stars by which I've sailed my luffing Chinese junk. And always, for nearly twenty rapt years, I thank my loving, beloved, and forgiving wife Cyndi, who with me steers through the dusty, glowing, black, and boundless cosmos and this mere book—my words and her visual art. Living on in a community of memory and hope with decency and empathy in the face of eventual loss gives us great measure of power and joy.

Tom Vander Ven
Atlanta, Georgia

INTRODUCTION

The title of Tom Vander Ven's book announces a ghostly theme in the form of a stage direction: [*Enter Ghost*]. That he uses a stage direction as the title isn't surprising. His career as a writer has been closely associated with the dramatic arts, and two of the major entries in this book are plays. For many years, before setting out on the extensive peregrinations of what some people call "retirement," he wrote and directed plays for the South Bend Civic Theatre, an institution that matured into a staple of local cultural life during his time in association with it. Yet the title of his book is more than a reference to a literary convention, recalling the incipient event in Shakespeare's *Hamlet* when the ghost of Hamlet's father appears before the castle watchmen, Bernardo and Marcellus, and their compatriot Horatio, a skeptical scholar. In a collection that contains plays, but also stories, essays, and poems, Vander Ven shapes a unifying theme focused on a problem of time and memory, and of perception, that can be understood in ghostly terms. It is a haunted and haunting book, because it shows us the strangeness of our familiar lives—lives in which we ourselves sometimes move as ghosts through time.

The title captures the complexity of the general problem of our relationship to aging, to death, to the voices that speak to us in memory and from the grave, from the unwritten history of our secret losses and from the written histories that continue to haunt us because they seem somehow unfinished or provisional.

We shall revisit the famous scene from *Hamlet*; but we should first note that [*Enter Ghost*] is a title that makes ambiguous utterances at the same time that it alludes to the history of ghosts in dramatic literature, inviting a rethinking of that older literary tradition.

A stage direction directs the actors but also informs them, showing them (and the reader) what happens in the play that they must imagine and imitate. We hear a constative utterance: *Here, now, a ghost enters*. But the phrase "Enter Ghost" is not simply a command given to actors or a description of action. It may be an utterance addressed to the ghost itself. Either an imperative: *Enter, ghost.* Or an invitation: *Please enter, dear ghost.* Or an incantation. Even a prayer: *Come to us, O Ghost!* Where and how shall the ghost enter? Will we make possible an entrance for the ghost?

Opening this book, we find ourselves in the presence of ghosts. We lose ourselves in the presence of ghosts, which are themselves only markers of an absence. Losing ourselves, we may become ghosts. And so it is possible to hear the command as also addressed to us, inviting us into the book: *Enter, as the ghost.* Perhaps every work of literature makes this conditional demand: *If you are a ghost, enter here.* Every reader of a book is a ghost haunting its passages.

But there is at least one other macabre resonance. The phrase may be directed to the reader in another sense. As readers, we are invited to enter [the] ghost, to enter the ghostly realm of this text. Every book title is an invitation to read, and this one is perhaps also a dare. Is the author challenging us, like the barker at a carnival? "Twenty-five cents. Walk through the dark door you see before you and enter into another world." Is the book itself the ghost?

Do we enter the ghost? Do we enter and become the ghost? In order to enter, must we already be ghosts? The title implicates us.

In this digital age, it is hard to ignore yet another insinuation, namely, that we sit before the book as before a computer screen, and a dialog box pops up to prompt us: *Enter Ghost.* Type "ghost" into the search box, and thereby enter the ghost virtually. "Ghost" is the pass-word. To proceed with your purchase, please enter "ghost." Ghosts, after all, are a manifestation of virtual reality. The ghost isn't real in the same sense that we are; and yet, by welcoming the ghost and giving the ghost voice, we enter into the world of the ghost, we give ourselves a second life. There is always another window, each one a ghost of the other. In this book they proliferate, not only in texts, but also in images, collages that combine references from many sources and reshape them, images that converse with the texts rather than illustrating them. At the same time that this collection employs traditional forms, it dem-onstrates an awareness of new ways of reading, of navigating texts in a virtual realm and altering them to suit our needs. These possibilities involve us in risks. What is the ghost? Whose ghost? Where does it come from? Upon what scene does it enter? What demands does it make? What is our responsibility here?

In *Hamlet*, just before the ghost enters, Horatio expresses his skepticism regarding such supernatural occurrences: "Tush, tush, 'twill not appear." Horatio speaks as a scholar, a rationalist. He only knows what his science tells him is possible. Hamlet, himself hardly a superstitious thinker, will later admonish Horatio: "There are more things in heaven and earth, Horatio, / Than are dreamt of in your philosophy." In this book, Tom Vander Ven takes up this same corrective role with us. We may no longer credit the existence of "actual ghosts," but this does not mean that there is nothing overwhelmingly and threateningly strange in our world, nothing to invade our imaginations and haunt us as effectively as the ghosts of old; nor does it mean that we aren't, in our own way, subject to being ghosted.

In the most overt example in [*Enter Ghost*], the nineteenth-century politician Schuyler Colfax appears in Vander Ven's short play "Now Like a Dream" and is eventually revealed to be a ghost. His wife, Ellen, is in the process of composing a letter when Schuyler appears in the doorway. What follows, however, is an ordinary domestic exchange, not a scare, not a haunting. In fact, Schuyler begins simply by asking his wife, "Are you all right?" In this way, the play undermines traditional expectations. The ghost is much like a memory. Schuyler Colfax, as a ghost, carries on with the topics that had engaged him in life. We get the sense that this is the ordinary course of life and death—that death is a continuation of life, and that people (perhaps especially historically significant people) continue to pursue their objectives in their conversations with the living, in the way they occupy our thoughts. But Vander Ven also makes of Schuyler Colfax, the Vice President who left Washington under a gauzy cloud of scandal, a spokesperson for the future, an enthusiastic reader of Walt Whitman's *Leaves of Grass*. He is someone who, despite his fixation on the past and on writing and revising his own life story, is drawn to a discourse that points America toward the post-civil rights movement era. A dead man reads a book and is transformed by it. Or are we to take this conversation between husband and wife as a memory, as a conversation Ellen revisits—and in that sense is haunted by—from her recent past? In that case, we are encouraged to consider the extent to which all of the experiences we have had together continue to resonate in us. The spouse we have lost returns, interrupts us, has always something more to tell us. We continue to live together. Essentially nothing has changed. Which is to say, we continue to change one another. This is certainly the nature of history: the past is still being written; it is still being lived.

The problem of time and memory, and the question of individual survival, is made more complex in this volume's second play, *The Vandalia Cat Murders*, a drama without ghosts, but one that is all the more ghostly for that. Vander Ven captures, once more in a dialogue between elderly spouses, the spectral nature of communication. In the life of Harold and Margaret, repetition becomes a kind of ghost, haunting their conversations. The old self, the time-worn stance and attitude, returns again and again, confronting the interlocutor with the mysterious monument of the other's ego, each character the instrument of a prescribed program that began years ago. People are, first of all, myths. We are the stories we tell ourselves about ourselves, hoping meanwhile to persuade (and possibly vanquish) others. Vander Ven expresses the problem succinctly in an autobiographical segment of the mixed genre piece "[Enter Ghost]": "In the 1940s, I began to notice me noticing me but only vaguely sensed it as an aura out of which I would begin to tell me about myself in stories." People who live together live with one another's ghosts. Harold refers to Margaret's habits of privacy as ghostly. She disappears. She is only upstairs, in her private room, but what is she doing? The question has haunted him for years. By definition (despite his later investigations), he can't know. Tellingly, their foundering marriage only rights itself and sails on after he and Margaret have bailed enough bilge water to at last acknowledge their mutual inability to penetrate to some inner truth at the heart of the other's mystery.

Much of the work before us was written "in retirement" and concerns retirement. Retirement, Vander Ven says, is a kind of disappearing. The retired person, like the elderly person in general, becomes more and more invisible to society at large. In retirement, a hard-to-welcome aura of anonymity descends upon us. At times it becomes possible to live a posthumous life, to see and speak as if from the other side of the grave, the dark, cold, earthy side, beneath the leaves of grass. This may seem like an awful fate. (It is!) But it can lead, as our author demonstrates, to the acceptance (at least now and then) of a strange and ghostly freedom, a new life backstage at the theatre of the ego.

The present moment, what is left of our youth, of our life, is fleeting. Of course! We easily acknowledge the fact. But it is our secret denial of the loss that makes it so easy for us to nod our heads. Meanwhile, "Voices of gulls call through [us] on the wind; / the dog circles out beyond our voices" ("Sea Washes Sand Scours Sea"). Other people are waking elsewhere and in other times. Some of those people are us —an infinite number. Others (an even greater infinity) can't remember us, can't imagine us. Past, present, and future: like the sublime otherness of the Arenal Volcano, they obliterate us.

Right now we are together, this miraculous day. Nevertheless, "The day does not diminish other days." This is a good thing: to welcome the future; not to take revenge upon the past; to permit the other his or her unaccountable life in the present, to welcome the one whose question ("Why are you like that?") challenges the truth of our own most comforting stories.

But today, how comforting not to be ghosts (we who are already ghosts)!

Joseph Chaney
Lille, France

-][-

All the new thinking is about loss.
In this it resembles all the old thinking.
—*"Meditation at Lagunitas," Robert Hass*

Samira Emilie

DREAMS OF SPEED

The street ran south for three
blocks and all downhill past
snow-buried houses the pavement packed
hard and bright under street light
through the bare trees
in our little town as we
ran stumbling the red runners
slamming against our legs until
we threw ourselves hard
onto the ice our sleds flying
past the Reverend Mr. Crystal's house
through icy air and dreams of speed
down to where the street curled
to the road that ran beside the great grain
elevator and we sailed our sleds high
into the country fields deep in snow
under a black sky
filled with old stars.

old stars
grew large
floated above my bed

Ed Brandt

Breathe Once Before the End

No news, no sighting,
no eyewitness report, no film clip,
no thing haunts me
like the hammer-footed beast
born in my eardrum
that skulked the halls
of the house I tried to fall asleep in
when I was ten, when I held my breath
grew large and floated above my bed,
filling the room until the beating stopped—
as I do rarely now at thirty-five.

Heidi Cobb

IONA THE DEVIL'S GIRL

I don't remember whether our mother warned us about anything before we started out for the 1948 Michigan State Fair along Eight-Mile Road and Detroit's Woodward Avenue of streetcar rails, electric cables, and traffic. And she was a worrier. Creeks. Silos. Polio. Milk trucks rolling along the town's highway a block away. Our World War II terrier, Ike, was the only family casualty of that traffic. Well, there was the fox that would become, posthumously, a family pelt. It ran in front of my father's car as he was driving home from the Chrysler Tank Arsenal. He published the town's weekly newspaper and during the war worked nights at the plant. When we got up that morning, the fox, propped up on a box beside our garage, looked alive.

My brother and I were ready for carnival rides and pig barns and sideshows. At the fair grounds, we entered a dimension unlike anything I'd ever traveled in my little-twerp mind, including a closet in the house on School Street where the chipped plaster statue of some hybrid mold of the Statue of Liberty and the Madonna appeared on the day we moved in, blessed us in glitter and blue and red paint and got me off to a luminous beginning in the first town I can remember. The Protestant Village of my Carnival Madonna had maybe two Catholics, one Jew, one displaced Japanese-American family from the state of Washington, and a Baptist minister who, before the war was over, stood accused of being a Nazi sympathizer. Someone claimed to have seen in the church basement a red flag with a swastika.

What's the appeal of hay, straw, road apples, and cow pies? We town-boys swam through the fertile aromas of state fair barns filled with cattle, horses, sheep, and pigs, inhaling the sweet, foul swirl of dung and cotton candy on our way past pigeons and scattered popcorn to the carnival rides—the Whip, Dodgem, and Ferris wheel, the hustlers and ride drivers, and the mindless, festival mechanics of a player-calliope whistling carnival tunes through perforated rolls of music. We wanted to throw baseballs at milk bottles and rise up rockingly over the tents and freak shows on the death-defying, clattering wheel of girders and bolts.

Bobby Huff climbed the town's water tower that summer, *a cappella,* clambering up the erector set to stand atop the tank and wonder, "Now what? What next?" Someone saw him jump around and wave his arms. From the tower he might have looked down at the vacant band shell in the little park or beyond the stoplight to the unknelling steeple of the Congregational Church. On his way down, did his foot slip, his grip fail? He brushed past an unnerved kid who hadn't made it to the top. The sod beneath the tower absorbed some of the impact, and he was still moving a little when people arrived. Dr. Burley came from his house across Saint Clair Street and closed his eyes.

Before he killed himself, he wandered into our backyard where I was playing in a sandbox with Dwight Stanlake. Bobby stepped into the sandbox, kicked cars off their roads, and leveled hills. My mother told him to leave the yard. "Now what? What next?" A frayed thread, unspooling. Everybody talked about it for weeks, but nobody said anything. He was from some other town, visiting his aunt.

Nobody ever really said anything about death that made a difference. You fell off a water tower into the arms of Jesus. You fell off a dead log into a green pond and into the lap of the Lord. Some of us boys went together to the hushed room at the funeral home across the street to see what was left after drowning. Mickey Winkler just lay there, wearing his face like a painting or a towel. I looked from way across the room where it felt safe. I thought—when you die, you're a window display, and all the shoppers pass by. They slow down, stop, look stupefied, and move on. But nobody admits anything. They just say you're in a better place. *So stop staring at me. I'm not going to tell jokes or ride a bike or apologize. I'm not coming back.*

At the university hospital in Ann Arbor, I worked the weekend midnight shifts on my way to an 8 a.m. Spanish class where I routinely pitched forward about forty-five degrees before regaining consciousness of conjugations and "un sandwich de queso." On-call orderlies pushed gurneys down dim hallways to freight elevators to the sub-basement morgue's refrigerator doors. But first, always—as in ALWAYS—check the room number—as in 11-B—and check the name eleven times before you go into the room to get the body. Don't try to tag the toe of a sleeping patient. Or wrap gauze around its jaw. It wakes up. You'll wish you were flipping burgers on the day shift at Crazy Jim's. Once you know it's dead, then it's doable. If it's a child, stack blankets and towels on top to make it look like laundry. And act like it's laundry when you push past visitors.

The evanescence of Ferris wheels. It's mostly the anticipation. The carnival's revenge. Jack wanted the wheel to stall while we were on top and scare the pants off us. Maybe they'd have to send someone up with food and a can to pee in. We looked around at the smell of the city's distance. At the silence of the ants. And then we were back on earth, heading for the next gaudy wonder, the sideshows with the two-headed baby, the world's smallest woman, and a crocodile with the head of a man.

I had no idea what was under the red fur, hanging by a rope from a rafter in Biff Baumgartner's garage. We swarmed like flies. Biff was a magician, his knife unzipping the skin, peeling it away in one aimless length of tail and legs. Muscle, membrane, teeth, and tongue crawled out into a thin, gleaming, pink fox. All along, an unseen light had been shining beneath the red fur. When we die, we get smaller and glow. Like the monstrous black bear hanging from the Standard Oil sign that winter, glittering in the indifferent snow. Then, unpelted, beheaded, rendered. No one said that they saw themselves or god skinned, hanging from a garage's rafter.

The sideshow men with voices like auctioneers sized us up to believe that we were about to buy the cosmic, real thing, the exposed, deformed, living world-of-flesh, in what turned out to be large jars of soaking, peeling, white fetuses, pickled circus miscarriages. I thought that maybe under the ghostly, fetal skin it might have something to do with death.

In a rocking, clattering train across the brute December snowfields of Michigan, four years before, I rode with my mother to Holland, where Grandpa George had had an accident. The businessman, the blacksmith, the Dutch army veteran, the immigrant who read Plato

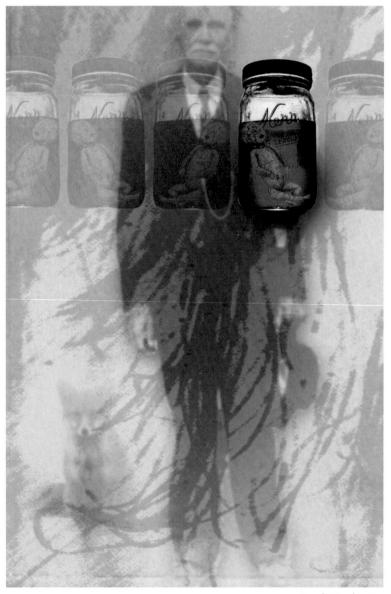

Cyndi Vander Ven

and Spinoza and who forbade his daughters to speak Dutch or to read the lurid novels of Thomas Hardy, hidden in their dresser drawers where no man might go. This hammerer of fishing spears. This man brought down by sidewalk ice, in bed in the great stone Ninth Street house near Kollen Park, with pneumonia, white-mustached and frail, flattened by blankets. He knew my name. He smiled and asked me how I was and then died, posed at home in a parlored casket, wearing his wire-rimmed glasses, grave and answerless, and just beneath his tight skin something like a skull.

Wild, black hair coiled around the red sign above us. Snakes stared. *Iona the Devil's Girl. Child of the Jungle. From the remote forests of the Amazon. Silent, mysterious child of dark rivers. Her parents unknown. Her world undiscovered. Dare to see her here today. What few have ever seen before. Gaze into her eyes. Iona. The Devil's Girl. Begin the journey now. Twenty-five cents. Walk through the dark door you see before you and enter into another world. Iona's world.*

What was it like to walk out of Michigan through that sullen arch into the land of the child of dark rivers? Jack and I were National Geographic-style drugged virgins at the edge of a volcano. Until that day, the most exotic girl I had ever seen or thought about was Norma the Neighbor's Girl, with braids, one blue eye, and one brown eye. Now Iona the Devil's Girl silently beckoned. Really. Summoned. Compelled. But to do what? Through a black curtain we entered, maybe twenty people, a large oval arena with a low wall around it, like a small hockey rink, and a white canvas floor with snakes everywhere. Nothing but snakes. None of them were coiled. None of them moved.

In the middle of the floor, on a metal folding chair, a figure sat with her back to us. It had to be Iona herself. Long, black, straight hair fell nearly to the floor. A blanket of immemorial colors wrapped itself around her shoulders and legs. She leaned back in the chair with her extended legs covered and her bare, brown feet exposed. Motionless, displayed, and concealed. With her snakes, a traveling jungle tableau. We had no idea what we were looking at. She was probably alive. Aware of us? Maybe. But there was no jungle welcome. The guide in blue jeans and a green T-shirt was silent. We were on our own in Iona's shabby, wordless court of anticlimax. Jack counted the money in his pocket. Now what?

Ladies and gentlemen, you have traveled into Iona's distant land of darkness, of lurking reptiles and strange silence. But the journey doesn't end here. We now go farther into the dark jungle where Iona lives. To look on the face of Iona herself, the very face of darkness, the face of the Devil's Girl, we have to cross to the other side. For twenty-five cents, you can gaze on the face of Iona, into the eyes of darkness itself, the Amazon, the monster crocodiles that infest its waters. See into her eyes, into the dark world.

It was Jack's money. His paper route. He bought our tickets to the other side. The crowd thinned as we moved around to watch Iona reveal herself. At first, all we could see was more black hair, covering her face. We stood safely behind the necessary wall, waiting for something to happen, for Iona's hair to open like the curtain on the high school stage. Then her hands rose slowly out of the blankets, and her hair began to move and spread like the wings of a dark bird. In the light's gloom, I began to see that Iona wore brown skin, heavy-lidded, dark eyes, a full, solemn mouth, and a wide nose and nostrils. But she had no face. She seemed to be erased. Iona, if she was ever a girl, was not there for me to see. This life of panting forms and auras dies into unspeakable silence, dim and blank and pitiless, stripped bare, rendered, blanketed, by ritual and display made diminishingly whole. The art of dying. Or to watch, dying. Wordless.

to watch, dying
wordless
swinging a tire

NELLIE WHITE'S PARTY

I'm five today, lying here, swinging a tire that hangs from the ceiling. My mother sits on the edge of the bed. She doesn't say anything about my hairy arm or my big thumb. I can hear the calliope whistling happy birthday to me through the bars of the circus wagon.

"What are you doing?"

"People on the ground can only see my arm because I'm flat on my back. Gargantua the Great."

"Did your friends have a good time at the circus?"

"Guess so. What does he think about all day?"

"What he thinks about I'm sure I have no idea. Probably just another day in the Greatest Show on Earth."

"Are all the gorillas in cages?"

"And zoos. Or in the wild. In Africa. Maybe he thinks about Africa."

"He wasn't watching the planes."

"What?"

"Flying over. P-38 Lightnings."

"They must be flying out of Selfridge Field."

I ask her to tell the story again of her little town in western Michigan, when she was ten, when she heard the far-off cough and buzz of an engine and looked up to see her first airplane. Now it's 1942, and we have an aircraft spotters guide with silhouettes, cruising ranges, engine specs, and armaments. We keep our eyes on the sky. Stukas. Junkers. Messerschmitt 109s at nine o'clock.

She always says there are no German aircraft over Almont or any other American town or city. The Axis will not bomb apple orchards anyway. I should try to relax so sleep will come. We sing "Now the Day is Over," "—night is drawing nigh, shadows of the evening steal across the sky." Bombers drone across the bedroom ceiling. I blink at the night like a toad.

"If you close your eyes and rest, you'll go to Nellie White's party." As though I've been invited. "Go to Nellie White's party." Where would I go? Down some dim stairway to a dark landing, knock a timid knock till a door opens slowly, and a frail, disembodied voice says, "Come in. We've been waiting for you." A tiny table with four chairs, small saucers and cups. No one is in the room. Or there is no room.

But if my mother's right, Nellie will greet me like an aunt in an apron. She'll give me a hug and a plate of cookies, maybe meringues. Refuge from the sleepless dark in a warm, lighted parlor. But the party scares me. Who's waiting on the other side of the darkness? I never find out from my mother who Nellie White is, and I never go to the party, but out of the shadows over the years, Nellie, Nell, and Ellen come to me.

When Nellie is still a child, her mother hears voices, fears poison in her perfume bottles, and spends years in the Lapeer State Home. Even though Nellie keeps a picture by her bed, she doesn't think the young woman is her mother. When she's sixteen, her father dies on volunteer duty, fighting a fire in a grain elevator. She leaves school to manage the family hardware store where she has worked since she could read labels. She cuts and threads pipe and mixes paint, and she knows the price per pound of every nail and screw in the store. On the pocket of the smock she wears the stitched name her father called her—"Nell."

She cuts her straight, brown hair to taper downward so when she leans forward to sew or to read, it frames, like a nun's wimple, her high cheekbones and large gray eyes. When she talks, she tends to look aside, at times through her hair. Her lips are very expressive, as if she could speak in other languages with nuance. People think she understands them even when she isn't listening.

A neighbor who wants to paint her kitchen opens a book of colors on the paint department's counter. "Oh, Nellie, you have too many colors here. I don't know how to choose."

"Close your eyes and tell me the color you see. Tell me where you've seen it or how you imagine it, and I'll find a way to mix it. Start with anything that you see."

"Cantaloupe."

"Do you see it?"

"I smell it. Very sweet." She touches her fingers to her throat. "The seeds are spilling out in the sink. From Hanna's garden."

"Hanna's wearing her smock."

"Always." And Rebecca leaves with two cans to paint her sewing room where she'll sit often, not sewing, looking into the distance, soft orange and blue pouring into her eyes. Her husband thinks she has spells. She doesn't see him standing in the doorway.

People talk with Nellie expectantly, though her tone only hints at other meanings. They walk away, hearing some suggestion in her voice. Or they watch her walk away, wide shoulders on a thin body, her steps exotic, toes turned slightly outward as if poised to dance down the hardware aisles of her exile. Sometimes she wears her oversized smock like a toreador's cape.

Which she swirls one day as the dentist, dry-skinned Dr. Hawley, comes in for light bulbs. "What would you do if Rhett Butler walked into this hardware store? I'll bet he'd sweep you off your feet."

"Would his intentions be honorable, doctor?" Nellie turns away, arranging on a shelf some cans of 3-in-one oil.

He smiles with a glance at her ankles, "Oh, yes, I'd see that he treated you well."

"Your sense of duty?" She gives him a long sideways look through her hair, as if to wait for his answer. He steps backward, almost bowing.

"Well, then, Nellie, yowza, yowza, yes, ma'am."

When she visits her father's grave, she takes a cloth bag with a pair of scissors and a rag rug from a wooden box inside the back door of her house. In the box with the scissors are twine, string, and small seed packets of carrots, beets, and lettuce that she will plant in her victory garden during the war. On the rag rug she kneels to trim the grass around his headstone in the Sandhill Cemetery, not far from stones of the past century's graves—Burton, Culver, Ferguson. She lives with ghosts of memory, talking softly in her father's ear.

In April, 1942, on the day her boyfriend Jimmy Brown goes to the army, he comes around the counter of the hardware store to kiss her goodbye. As he leaves, Nellie turns her face against the ladder along the high wall of wooden drawers of bolts, screws, and nails. She thinks she'll never see him again because life is a leaving, person by person, into shadow and silence.

His letters home to "My dearest Ellen" describe the lunge and roll of an unnamed troop ship on an ocean crossing, restless days without names, the white light glaring off the waves. He asks how the Tigers are doing and will she please believe that he will come home to her. She writes seasonal stories to him about the sweet smell of ripe apples, the red and golden leaves of the orchards, the first dust of November snow, and through the long nights of Michigan winter the hopeful hymns of Christmas. Her letters continue their slow crossing of the Atlantic long after he vaults from a landing ship onto the beachhead at Anzio in 1944, struggles ashore through the foam, and dies instantly in an artillery barrage.

Jimmy's mother gives Nellie a photograph of her son in uniform that will stand on the fireplace mantel in Nellie's home for the rest of her life. The neighbor's son who shovels the snow from her sidewalk over the next few winters thinks it's the smiling western movie star Roy Rogers. He tells his friends, and they want to help him shovel snow.

In the years after the war, Nellie begins to imagine herself as a pilgrim lover. She reads about Rome, Pompeii, and the invasion of Italy; she sets money aside. Norman Kuhn works for her, silently worships her, and doesn't realize that she's grooming him to manage the hardware store while she's away.

She sails in September of 1951, stays the first night in a small hotel in Rome near the Termini, and walks around the Piazza della Repubblica the next morning. She pauses to watch the photographing of a young woman passing through a gauntlet of men. One man sits on a motor scooter, eyeing her, his head cocked like a bird. Another, leaning on his umbrella, croons some flirtation, mostly to impress the other men. An elderly man, his jacket worn like a cape, sees in the woman the gone beauty of his wife who stands that morning on a balcony above an empty, narrow street, smoking a cigarette and thinking about the son who vanished in the wastelands of war. Nellie has read that Italian men are aggressively amorous. The young woman passes by the same men a second time. Another photograph. As she walks toward the Via Nazionale, Nellie keeps one hand inside her purse.

The next day she takes a train to Nettuno, checks into a hotel, and under a warm June sun walks from her hotel to the military cemetery where Jimmy lies beneath one of thousands of white crosses. As she enters an arc of graves, she measures her steps so that her left foot falls just at the head of each cross. From Jimmy's mother she has already learned the location of his row and marker and kneels on an embroidered towel to touch the cross. From her purse she takes a very large nail and presses it deep into the soil beneath the grass. During the day she walks through the cemetery, memorizing names.

When the cemetery closes at 4 p.m., she has hidden herself behind shrubs, and at dusk she returns to her vigil beside Jimmy's grave, reciting his entire row and the rows that surround him. She sleeps that night wrapped in a shawl beneath the bronze and fresco maps of the invasions of Sicily and Italy and returns at dawn to sit beside the grave. The second morning a gardener finds her asleep.

The superintendent of the cemetery arranges for a taxi to take her to her hotel where she eats in the little dining room without seeing her food, saying silently the list of the dead. The waiter watches her go to her room. Later that night he lets himself in, puts a hand over her mouth, then the other between her legs. Nellie bites him, clamping down like a terrier, and stabs an awl into his wrist. The next morning Nellie nods when the desk clerk hopes she has had a good stay. On her walk to the train station, a passing parade celebrates Santa Maria Goretti, the eleven-year-old virgin of Nettuno who a half-century before resisted the sexual assault of a farm worker who stabbed her repeatedly. She forgives him before she dies.

Home in Michigan, when Nellie thinks of Jimmy's grave, she smells bread and tastes salt. Since she was a child, sleep has not come easily. She lives her life in the shadows of memory and imagination, hearing every strange noise in the house far into the night as she reads through the fiction shelves of the town library. *The Marble Faun. The Portrait of a Lady. A Farewell to Arms.* At three in the morning she slides into slippers and pads to the bathroom to wash the odor of book dust from her fingers. At seven she awakens to another day on the old oak hardware floors like a labyrinth of dreams in which every aisle turns to another aisle of paint and solvents or rakes and shovels or bulbs, switches and outlet covers.

Her Italian pilgrimage grows out of wistful memory—Jimmy's vow that he would come home to her. Every October beside his grave she reads to him as if he were falling asleep or as if he has become restless. She kneels in the Mediterranean sun beneath a parasol and reads passages she has marked for him.

> Red lips are not so red
> As the stained stones kissed by the English dead. . . .
> Weep, you may weep, for you may touch them not.

Risk, ruins, and memorials to loss draw her to Italy. In Nettuno she stays at the same hotel, but she never sees again the waiter with the stigma on his right hand. In Rome she stays always at the same little hotel off the Via Nazionale and spends hours gazing through the vastness of the basilica of Santa Maria degli Angeli e dei Martiri. She studies Bianchini's bronze meridian line and stands in the thin beam of sun that pierces a small hole in the towering wall to mark along the line the planet's orbit through solstice, Easter, and equinox.

At the Protestant Cemetery—which "might make one in love with death"—Nellie reads that Keats's name was "writ in water," and she thinks of the beach at Nettuno. The vibrance of the Roman streets plays unnoticed across the scrim of her imagination. She does not listen to the music in the piazzas or to the laughter and arguments of those living in the narrow streets. Her hand rests on the sleeve of remembrance.

In the dim front window of Nellie's home hangs a black and white photo of a field of crosses. Beside it hangs a small banner framed in red and white. At its center a gold star floats in a dark field of blue. This is her work. There are no gold star flags for lovers. No one in town disputes her losses. In ashamed silence, the men have fantasies in which Nellie invites them to her house in the middle of the night and undresses slowly in a seductive ballet. They imagine that her hardware smock conceals a full, womanly figure.

These are small threads in the web of the cosmos. We adorn and imagine, lie and create, the breathed biology of our births and deaths. Had my mother sitting on my bed revealed Nellie as the unbeatified Virgin of Michigan, there would have been no party for me to never attend. Had my mother adorned the party with her own fears and wishes, I might not have been able to open the door into Italy. Or out of Africa.

Gargantua the Great dies in 1949 of pneumonia, ending twelve years of caged celebrity and gaudy isolation. Though he lives before the laboratory era of inter-species sign language, Nellie teaches him some version of hand talk. I introduce these two-of-a-kind at one of her parties for insomniac adults.

"Miss Nellie, I'd like you to meet my friend, Mr. Buddy. Buddy, this is my childhood friend, Miss Nellie White." She takes his hand politely but warily. Is the awl close by? She closes her other hand over his. He doesn't pull away.

"Your hand is gentle, Mr. Buddy." She smiles, but he doesn't make eye contact. He's looking sidelong at the plate of cookies.

"Maybe you'd like to have one?"

"I wouldn't offer him the whole plate to choose from."

So here he sits cross-legged on the floor, all 450 pounds, sniffing at a cookie on a napkin in one hand. It's so small he can snort it up a nostril.

"I feel as though I know you," Nellie says. "You were with the circus. You're Gargantua." She moves her chair a little closer but turns it so that she's not looking directly at his scarred face. How does she know? Her hand is on her knee, and he turns his head almost imperceptibly to look at her white skin. Beyond the aroma of the cookie Buddy smells this woman and the orchards of Michigan. And metal fittings. And paint.

I don't tell her about how he was an orphan at one month and raised by missionaries or about the acid attack that twisted his mouth into a snarl. Lots of people ride a freight train of abuse and wasted days. But she doesn't ask any more about the circus years. She lives in the stillness of exile.

"Why don't you come visit me, Mr. Buddha? Stay with me for a while."

She doesn't ask my opinion. Like I'm not there, like I'll never sleep. Nellie teaches him a sign language for hardware—nail, broom, and wrench. He works part time in the store, and she has to train him not to put screws and washers in his mouth. She doesn't dress him up like a clown with a baseball hat that says "Buddy." He is the unadorned Hairy Alpha, her gorilla consort, rending and darkening the fantasies of the men of Rotary and Kiwanis.

At Nellie's house he has his own room with towels, blankets, and cushions. She builds for him an oversized porch swing, double-chained, where he swings for hours with Mimi, a stuffed, one-eared bunny. Buddy likes bedtime stories and the rhythms of Nellie's voice. He leafs endlessly through picture books—petting primates, penguins, cats, and dogs.

She weaves stories, one of them about Georgio, an Italian gorilla who plays the guitar. No one knows where he took lessons, but one morning in Rome he appears on a step at the base of the Bernini elephant on the Piazza della Minerva, improvising variations on a theme from *La Bohème*. A young woman who works in a nearby art supply store is walking languidly by during one of those long Roman afternoons when every store's door says "CHIUSO." Time sways in brilliant plumes of bougainvillea from old city walls. She begins to sing softly, "They always call me Mimi, I don't know why. Alone, I prepare my dinner."

Mi chiamano Mimì,
il perché non so.
Sola, mi fo
il pranzo da me stessa.

Georgio, a skilled accompanist, winds through her voice the strings of his guitar. Soon the Vespas and Fiats fall silent, the buses in the cross-town currents of the Via Vittorio Emanuele slow, and the tram on the narrow Via Arenula stalls beside the little Piazza Cairoli with its fountains of cascading pigeons and unfurling trees. The beggars rise above the Cairoli on their cardboard pallets and spiral like Fibonacci spirits into a canopy about the Minerva. Bewildered tourists emerging from the Pantheon consult their maps and guidebooks, but the people of the Centro Storico come out of their apartments and shops with folding chairs for an afternoon of opera della gorilla. "I pretended to be asleep because I wanted to be alone with you"—

> Sono andati? Fingevo
> di dormire perché volli
> con te sola restare.

That's how Buddy finds his way to sleep on my vigil, listening to Nellie's stories, sometimes with a towel cowled over his head or with Mimi tucked under his chin or snuggled against the shoulder of his Africa.

We come into the world in strangers' arms, primates of assorted hair and skins. We sleep in strangers' arms, grooming our beliefs and hugging our stuffed animals, restless under the stars till the end of knowing, when the circuses and cemeteries, the operas and nations, fall away, and we subside into another place of untroubled sleep, still as strangers among the dark pools and grasslands of the cosmos.

Sandy Brown Jensen

Skeletons Need Mirrors

You will find me less good than you dreamed,
the flesh torn away by glances,
the nerves a fluttering comic fringe.

You will find me less true than you believed,
neither ghost-shirted against fire,
nor quick-frozen, waiting for my time.

The bony words, marrowless,
gnawed smooth, chess white,
wired here in place,
supposed, grinning.

Nantanat Choisutcharit

FALL OF THE MONARCH

As if the world were tipping over
and all summer sliding into fall
the monarch butterfly falls southward
in September in the longest fall
of any leaf I know.

Monte Merritt

MESSAGES

I. She chose fiction for his birthdays,
but this time wrapped the green novel
without reading it, and he didn't tell her
when he found the note, using
its message as a bookmark, reading
it each time he opened the book:
Hi—Sorry I missed you.—Bob

II. We are not, she argued to herself,
and later on the phone to her mother
she said it again, how she found
the note in a novel about the Shaker,
Ann Lee. "We can't give up. We need
each other," she told the handwriting
analyst. "Whom else are we to turn to?"
She'd tell him how wrong he was:
"You spoil it for the rest of us, you coward!"
On a screen in the computer lab,
fingers all around, tapping, tapping,
in the voiceless space, she found the note:
We humans are wrong for each other.

III. At times when he thought it was deviant,
a gastronomic *erotikos*,
Amanda advised him to stuff it
with yogurt and pimientos,
which led to a book of recipes,
"For the Phallic Vegetarian,"
then to heady, southwestern fantasies
of harmonica-playing armadillos,
so he studied the meteorology of dreams,
this aficionado of tornadoes,

disdained her slights and innuendoes,
this matador of pecadilloes,
eschewed her polonaise of mayonnaise,
this conductor allegro con brio.
The note was his Rorschach and horoscope:
First, hollow an avocado.

IV. How far the note has traveled
in the travel book he can not tell.
From around the next bend in the river
a flycaster fishes a bottled message.
In an Aleutian ravine three thousand miles
from launch, a cannery worker finds
a weather balloon. Maybe, he thinks,
she is already dead, starved for love—
the usual. The book itself provides no clue:
a German officer, stranded in Tibet
through World War II, drinks Yak butter tea,
hears tales of levitation, makes a face
at the thought of a yeti with a rock
in its hairy pocket. "But I believe you,"
says a shaved monk, "when you tell me
there are people that live in the great birds
that pass across the sun." The first time,
he leaves flowers on the shelf
beside the book, a handful of daisies.
Nothing. What do I expect, he grumbles,
this is a test. It's supposed to be hard.
He waits eleven days to buy carnations
from a Malaysian street vendor.
In nine more days, he smuggles
a dozen blood-red roses into the library
in an attaché case. Now he leaves a note
on saffron paper. What do you say
to a vision from Flint, to a home

economics teacher from Bakersfield?
The first draft begins, "I still care. I always will.
There was never anybody else."
The archivist who reads the notes nearly cries,
sees him watching her under an exit sign,
walks the other way, circles round
to intercept him. They take her coffee break
together, eager, full of awkward explanation.
Neither one thinks lovers should give ultimatums:
If I don't get flowers and poems from you,
I'll get them from somebody else.

V. Cross-legged, Jane sits for hours, humming
oh yes, oh yes, breathingly, oh yes, dozing
away into transcendent naps, remembering
her mother's soft voice waking her, and then
she wakes to the falling of her face, her hair
leaping at her neck's lash, and climbs up
out of the deep cramp of sitting still
to limp three steps, one foot sound asleep,
to slump to the floor, lost, massaging
the numb ankle till she can feel the pain.
"I hurt it meditating," she tells her dentist.
"Don't ask, okay?" Later a dull mandibular ache
mutters its own mantra while she tries
to dissect the sentence on the slip of tissue
that slides from a much-thumbed issue
of Discovery in the waiting room. She moves
the first three words to the middle, to read so:
"You will not change until you understand
you will not change." "Oh no!" And the fan
in her furnace keeps whispering oh no,
oh no, till she mails the tissue back
to the dentist with a note— "This fell
from one of your magazines."

Until you understand
you will not change
you will not change.

VI. Some stories neither begin nor end,
as if chimpanzees write our history,
hairy fingers against keyboards,
chuckling messengers who knuckle
toward their yellow bicycles
to make their chimpy rounds,
some clutching notes full
of punctuation
or neat rows of spaces
or random poignancies—

Eventual love swims

levatorelevatorelevatorE

More woe than piano

EVERYBODY SENDS THEIR LOVE

Through her candle skin
the waitress Juliet glows,
and in her smiling teeth
he tastes an aging memory.
She holds the darkened restaurant
in the curving of her nose and chants
the specials of the day:
the black-finned shark breaks
the surface of the table while beneath
the cajun chicken scratches in the hard floor.

So the teacher sends a valentine,
hides inside its fold, scrawling his desire,
professes neither love nor passion, calls
it an appreciation, a thank you.

The next day comes the mail, stuffed red
with valentines: One sends its love big
with child. The woman says
she is four months and five pounds gone,
her lover isn't happy, his kids are grown,
this just isn't what he had in mind.

No, she won't be back in school.
Not for a while, anyway.
Just what I need, he says, one valentine
from the unborn, another from the undead,
some postal hugs to help me
through this brute divorce.

Armand Dembski

A Work of the Heart's Trying

It's one of those dreams
that as you wake, you see
yourself leaving and you feel
the going away of another you
as a shadow that was living
in the truth for a little while.

And you don't cry
for the person you have been, knelt
as you were on the floor, your head
in your old Aunt Mary's lap,
all of you feeling
the convulsion of goodbye.

She begins to cry too
and to the others in the room
you would give up the same grief gladly,
old regret pouring itself out. You look around
anyway for the other part of the tent pole
you were carrying, but as things in dreams do
it passes back to another tent
to get good use.

John S. DeFord

THE LAMP LEAKS LIGHT

All night into the neighboring sky the lamp leaks
light through the bedroom windows. In the sack now
four hours and holding, the bread of my face sags
into the pillow. The canned and frozen goods
of my body shift and settle into the right,
then left side of sleep. By five the lamp begins
to fill a gray space among the leaves,
does its job, goes out.

I sleep through some of it, turning
myself like an attendant nurse, easing
a shoulder, rolling my cage like a bingo basket,
twisting in place.
Let someone else get up.
Let the smokers go to work squinting.
Let the car doors thud.

FASCIA

In a building in Krakow, Poland,
there is a shell-thin sculpture by
Igor Mitoraj, a face so large it is
free-standing on the floor.

When the tour guide turns away
to tell someone the university's history,
I take my face off and put it on the floor.
I don't want to draw attention;
I just want it off. It is not found art.
Or lost. I set it on one cheek
so it will not roll across the old stones,
turning heads as it clatters by.

Rather than call the law,
which would draw the media
with photos of still another yellow
POLICE LINE — DO NOT CROSS,
the university officials meet hurriedly
to act in everyone's best interests.
They title the sculpture:
"Askance" (Anonymous Donor).
Not even a suspect, I am free to go.

I remember that I wore an eggshell face
when I was five, when I read aloud
from the Bible at family outings.
Aunt Esther picked book and chapter,
and my boy voice went forth and begat.
One day, many, many books after

Deuteronomy, and after the ninth book
of Tarzan, I stumbled across the Book
of Orgasm. You should have seen
my meringue face come off,
angelic, contorted, ecstatic:
"Sunday School Boy Survives
Ten Thousand Volts. Wants More."
Years later, my mother would regret,
"You were such a good little boy.
What happened?" She was asking me,
her pubic boy, to read to her
in my best holiday falsetto.

The second face had hair beneath it,
with armpits to match, and as I gazed
through the mirror again and again,
I saw that the hair grew. And it was good.
During this reign of my physiognomonia,
I was all hirsute appetite,
racing my metabolism
as if I were the very engine
of lubed perpetuity, a moon giant,
stalking a village virgin, the seats
of my Nash folded down into a bed—
love's ambassador to the Detroit suburbs.

The face of St. Horning, mostly tongue
and lips, finally got its uppance
when I married. The trail of the quest
grew cold, my skin dried to a dull potato,
but at picnics my salad face would still
look fresh, in the jubilation of croquet,
or on vacation under a cowboy hat,

humming western theme songs,
teeming like a television show.

The mâché of that face began to work loose
even as my son and daughter crept
like Lilliputians over my gross paternus.
I read them stories—of a Chinese duck
late for dinner, of an American bison,
hunted by Sioux children,
and I tucked them to bed with songs
of Windy Marias and riding ghosts.

"What's happening to your face,
Uncle Bob?" My nephew gaped,
as it fell under the iron weight
of duty and rang against the pavement
like a church bell. Everyone turned
to see if it might be their own face,
clanging in the street. "Fear not,"
I cried, dressed in an orange fright wig
and green clown shoes. "'Tis I,
finding true love at mid-life."
No one laughed.

Years after, on the century's edge,
I still recall my life as an epic text
in which I, the hero, did read.
Today my piecrust face feels
its chin on the floor. It is not
the last layer of an onion, not
the core. It is not one of Cubbins'
progressivist hats, first one
without even a feather, later ones

growing more feathers, finally
a crown crawling with jewels. No.
Today a face ages in its place,
thinks it is only a face,
but thinks it is the only face.

Akira Hashiguchi

Whether Joy Is Grounded

Whether the sidewise light of morning lies.

Whether the blackbird's epaulets
orange and yellow on the branch
bearing only color give enough.

Whether the river brown after the hard rain
merely pours soil into the dying lake.
Into the air a blue siren.
Out of the sycamore buds peeling.

John S. DeFord

LISTENING TO BASEBALL IN WYOMING

The radios are warming up in Sundance,
as he stands in the doorway, facing west
into an August afternoon of baseball,
and watches an antelope round second base
into a gulley and hold up as the throw
from deep right center one-hops into the sage.

On the porch of her summer memories, the sage
face of her father squint-listens from Sundance
to a voice in Cheyenne telling fans in the West
that Bunning's rubber band arm turns baseballs
into billiards, and a man can't get on base
when a cushion of air at the plate banks the throw.

"In those days," her father claims, "pitchers could throw
eleven innings to break a tie." The sage
blows all season on the wind in Sundance,
scenting the smell of peanuts in the west
and the white noise of the crowd, as the baseball
tocks hard off the announcer's voice, the bases

loading with the tying run at first base.
Kaline takes one strike as her father throws
his voice along the wires, "You think I'm dumb as sage,
don't you, fakecasting baseball into Sundance
from a studio without windows, buried in the West,
guessing the time it takes to throw a baseball

from left field to third? You call that baseball?
How fast can a jackrabbit run to first base,
and if the shortstop makes a wild throw
that sails for nine seconds into the sage,

don't think we can't figure out in Sundance
that you're just reading a teletype out West."

Then Kaline hits a reply that rocks the West
and orbits Devil's Tower. No lie, that baseball
rides the daily gale east of third base
into fair territory, crows burst from pines and throw
themselves into the air, coyotes leap over sage,
and snakes rattle applause in the dust of Sundance.

Costa Rica: Four Texts

January: Nine Degrees North

The spirit engine of the verano sweeps
off the shaggy peaks of the Monteverde, seizes
the leaf-slapping, branch-rattling forest
in its huge paws, pauses, veers, resumes
its Spanish whoosh, whistling salsa all night
through the eaves and the swaying chains, pours
down the cow-tumbling slopes, whirls, turns
finches to fandangoed fans, and unstrings the kiting hawks.

The souls of the mountain people, windblown
since birth, deaf to the interminable roar of wind,
of trees swept with applause, encore of encores,
their leaves unflagging flags, sleep on,
while their bodies pad to the baño at two
to pee, slip back inside their dreams
to merengue their lithe and fragrant lovers.

Meanwhile, in their dusky bungalows
and brown cabinas, the gringos groan
and shudder in their troubled sleep,
wake and stare at the branches beating
down the moonlight to the ground,
like incessant surf against volcanic sand,
which is the turbine surge of jets at lift-off,
till the gringos find themselves huddled in sacks,
homeless beneath some overpass, pressed
into their mattresses by the whine and roar
of city traffic; they think that they've lost everything
to the boulder-bowling, snake-knotting wind.

All is not lost. The monkey shepherd walks
the morning paths, unties the grateful snakes,

finds a troop of monkeys which the wind
has blown inside out during the howling
night. These capuchins lie helpless as pink fruit
till the herdsman rinses them in buckets
of warm saline, reaches inside to grasp them
under their hairy armpits, pulls steadily
till they pop out of themselves, joyful infants
who stagger in a kind of drunken waltz, scramble
up the nearest trees to puzzle on a branch
until the world comes back to them.

Some mornings even the herdsman has problems,
gets thrown into thorns by the booling, sweeling wind,
unscrews himself from a swarming bush, restarts
his usual day, while the wind blows words apart,
writes new, unauthorized vocabularies, swirls up
a sword which slices itself into rowds and drows
which the herdsman mixes with rice and beans
to feed the hungry monkeys. This is how
the summer wind blows in San Luis de Monteverde.

Jay Cagle

Volcan Arenal

Until the second day, I had expected just another Stone Mountain, Georgia, or a theme park, a Six Flags Over Costa Rica—another hyped object of the traveler's gaze, our cameras clicking, water bottles swinging. Take a hike, take a ride on the dead lava flow. Take home a T-shirt: Arenal, Costa Rica, with a gaudy drawing of an exploding cone. I was there.

The day we arrive, there is no mountain at all, only shrouding clouds, with brief, gray glimpses of the lower slopes. But by the afternoon of the second day, a clear Saturday morning, we hear the thunder of cracking rocks at the top—sharp, staccato explosions from the great, domed hole in the earth's crust, mounded 3,000 feet above where we students and faculty gawk and wonder at the 7,000-year-old enormity.

With the help of the trained eyes of Jim Whitney, our geologist, and Sandy Whitney, an erstwhile volcanologist-turned-anthropologist, we can discern near the summit the dark, sliding paths of rocks, pushed off the rim by rising magma to tumble down the slopes, crumbling as they roll, and lower down the footprints of larger boulders bouncing off our retinas. We really are here.

On this day, the volcano Arenal seems to have grown overnight. I grope for adequate vocabulary: immense, looming, primordial. I avoid the "awesome" of contemporary worship. I heap adjectives on top of Jim and Sandy's geological terminology: tectonic plate motion, pyroclast, magma, lava dome, subduction zone. We're working together down here to build a term-dome. Emily Dickinson wrote that "the brain is wider than the sky," but in the Berkshire Mountains, in Amherst and Mt. Holyoke, there are no active volcanoes.

Of course, Arenal hasn't grown overnight—much. The new rockslides are insignificant to the larger time-drawn picture. The longer I look, the less I get it. I don't know what I'm watching, and Arenal doesn't know it's being watched. The theory that the object we observe is changed by the act of observation itself seems comically, pitiably egocentric.

The evening of the second day, on the green slope of our hotel, I'm sitting in a lawn chair that could have come from Wal-Mart. I have screwed on my wide-angle lens, I have charged my iPod, and I have iced my drink. Fully visible in the dimming light, the cone mountain of Arenal grows slowly darker, backlit by the western setting sun. Then, as the sun drops below the clouds, the northwestern slope begins to glow dully, like tarnished, fading brass. Monet painted countless haystacks in subtly changing light. O'Keefe painted New Mexican mountains in innumerable shades of gray.

How do I articulate the gravitas of this evening? This is no magic mountain. What we have here is the molten, ashen, ancient, volcanic thing itself, sans special effects or hobbits. This hard, fistular protrusion, this mountainous fire pit, draws unto its elemental self a flow of endless bus and rental-car traffic, shoddy shirt-art, wood carvings, postcards, and pilgrim inns—the Lavas Tacotal Lodge and the Erupciones Inn. Endless, that is, until the next massive eruption requires the tourist industry in this part of Costa Rica to remarket the venue.

See how I am distracted from the thing itself? Arenal is not an especially old volcano, but 7,000 years ago it began its slow, doming doom and had a 5,000-year head start on the very short history of the Roman Republic. And here it still slumbers fitfully, spews its smoke and stone, a banked fire fueled by the earth's molten core.

Suddenly, a deep-throated roar erupts across the blue and blurring evening sky. A small, elderly woman appears on a balcony. "What is that?" she calls down nervously. "Arenal," I say, because I want a generous Arenalian abruption, a large and blazing rock to catapult from the volcano, arc into the insensate sky, and land in the field before me, scattering the terrified cows and horses. I watch, untouched. Arenal, despite its thunder on a cloudless day, stands immutably mute as a witness to human merit or mortality. Its implacable indifference casts it shadow on my orphaned, shoeless figure sitting in its shadow. I am eager and afraid.

But this is not a cautionary tale. Nothing happens here tonight that makes the news. Arenal coughs, gargles, slumbers again, but the presence of the past, clearing its volcanic throat, has my stricken attention.

It has nothing to say to me, no interest in my edification. I am bird, blade, boulder, blasted sensibility—too much chaos spilling onto the grounds of the hotel, so I turn to music, remembering some in which I can hide and deny, Alan Hovhaness's "Mysterious Mountain" symphonic poems. His "Hymn to Glacier Peak" begins to modulate my brain with its slow, luxuriant, orchestral reverence. A little more brave now, I move on to "Mount Saint Helens," with its tympanic eruption, followed by a bird-song lyric resolution. Backgrounded by music, trees will again grow on the blighted slopes. Others have returned to volcanoes and to sleeping mountains—composers, civil rights leaders, poets of England and New England. I am by no means the first to wait. Out of the darkness, the fire never comes.

On the third day, clouds lie gray and soak our morning. Arenal has vanished in the rain. At the observatory, we view photographs of past eruptions and a computer screen that displays the seismograph's tracking of tremors and sounds. While carnival birds swarm the feeding stations, a dozen coatimundis skitter across the lawn, hoping for dropped pieces of melon. One with an injured forepaw perches on the railing of the observation deck, poses with us for pictures but scurries off to chase a rival into the replanted forest. We hear more talk more of lava chambers and unpredictability. Jim tells us that Arenal is a volcano of moderate size and moderate activity. It sounds like a classical volcano of the Enlightenment. Despite the unpredictability, this neighborly moderation reassures me a little.

And yet, Arenal's moderate presence leads to an immoderate question: who is it that we humans think we are? On what ground of future tremor, shock, and volcanic upheaval do we make the claim of holy privilege and exemption from death? How do we make the case that a personal god has, perhaps, chosen the next day for a display of torrential lava flow or for an explosive, toxic, gaseous emission as our last wondering day on the earth's broken and shifting crust?

Samira Emelie

Magician Tree

I. The magician tree turns black
against the fading glass and flattens itself
to a curtain of the nocturnal mind,
teatro oscuro.

It does not know how to frighten
with its blank erase of half a heaven;
swelling blindness folds the veins
and saddled bark into a cloak
and riddle.

II. Tonight the tree plays an orchestral wind,
wipes retinal flashes across branches,
disguises sky, displays one numbered star,
some god's planet, the hunter's belt, wingtip
of the swan, remnants of winter fire
in a tropical sky.

III. The spinal tree balances a skull which stares
at the alleged bottom letters on an eye exam;
the small figures blink clear, then blur, the demise
of vision in the pale, starred light.
When the tree consumes the dying light,
how do we live with loss?
Sleep denies, provides.

Why Are You Like That?

"Why are you like that?" The tone doesn't accuse. But it's late evening, and Cyndi and I have been standing for ninety minutes on the street near the bus station in shabby downtown Quepos, waiting for a man from the rental car agency in San José to deliver a replacement rental car—one with air conditioning that works and with a roof that won't leak the hard rains of Costa Rica's green season.

In the dim light, his dark skin and thick, black hair obscure his face. He's small, thin, and stands very still. He may be twenty. Or thirty. He begins in a light, clear, polite voice, saying that he needs a job, that he's lost his passport. He wears a green and white soccer shirt, jeans, and carries a nylon bag. Over his shoulder on the other side of the street, an ant-line of red taxis crawls into the night. In the Restaurante Quepoa, a few people linger at tables. On stools at the counter, a man sits with a woman with long, blond hair, her head down on her arms. On the sidewalk in front of the restaurant, a man stands, a long police club hanging from his belt. On the back of his white shirt, SEGURIDAD.

"I need a job."

"No, señor. We don't have a job for you. No."

Cyndi says, "We're tourists. On vacation. We're just waiting for another rental car."

I flex my muscular street voice. "You don't need to talk to him. Don't give him any information."

"Why are you like that?" he asks me.

I built this voice in New York, Atlanta, Rome, and Milan, where I had stood in a train station, guarding our luggage, while Cyndi tried to find out on which binario our train would be leaving for Rome. A little girl (aren't they all gypsies?) begged insistently for money. "Sono povero, signor. Per favore, sono povero." It would always be the same first line written on their signs. I gave her a euro—"Grazie, signor"— and she walked away, but within seconds another girl (her sister?) appeared. "Sono povero, per favore, mangiare." Two thin girls with dark hair, in jeans and T-shirts—the street clothes of the planet—in voices of fervent, suffering supplication, a kind of moan and whine. I felt foolish, but not as foolish as when, in my stern professor's voice, I said, "No, no," and waved her away, whereupon she fell to the floor and began to kiss my shoe. She kissed my shoe. I felt like Yul Brynner in *The King and I*. No one's head shall be higher than mine. In the Milan train station.

"I came here to work, but I lost my passport. Can you help me?" I turn at a right angle from him.

Cyndi is more generous. "Your English is very good."

"I lived some time in the United States."

"Where are you from?"

"My home is in Nicaragua, but I lost my passport."

Again I say, "You don't need to talk to him."

"Why are you like that?" he asks. I turn to read his face. He looks at me steadily, like a kindly therapist, inviting me to explore my feelings. It's okay, he's saying. There's no force here, no threat. I am a human asking a human for help. This is not a difficult problem.

He's right, of course. Why am I like that? If a stray dog approaches me and sits up, begging, I check my pockets for biscuits. But with this mild, humiliated, desperate man, I'm all about protecting my wife, self-defense, about not giving money to some guy with a car parked around the corner and a home to go to after a good day of begging. So I turn away while Cyndi continues to talk with him.

"Where did you say you're from?"

"Nicaragua."

I watch him in the corner of my eye.

"What kind of work do you do?"

"My work is—" and he makes hacking gestures.

"Sugar cane? You cut sugar cane?"

"Si, sugar cane. I'm so hungry. I can't get work without a passport."

Cyndi turns to me. "He's not a beggar, he's not a street person."

On the Piazza di Minerva, in the July sun of Roman tourism, an old woman in a black dress holds out a cup, sweeping her arm from side to side as people with cameras and maps walked past. I lean in the shade of a building, while Cyndi buys an eraser in an art store. The gaunt beggar in sunglasses leans on a cane, shaking, her arms shaking, the cane shaking, the cup shaking. The skin on her face sags in intricate folds from her trembling skull, her gloved hands like the feet of birds, all toes, the nails protruding from snipped glove tips.

Her shaking increases as she holds out her cup, and she begins to stagger, her balance shifting, her body swaying to stay upright, almost toppling, until at times she seems to move in some ancient dance rhythm of the dying. This is my end, this is my last dance, on the trembling axis of a dying globe, on the vias of the centro storico. Do you turn from my ruins? Do you deny me?

I maneuver through the walkers, drop three coins in her clattering cup, and return to my shaded wall. An Italian in a doorway smiles at me. Such kindness. Small sacrifice. That morning, on my way to the kiosk for the morning *Il Messagero*, I had given my ritual one-euro tribute to the jazzy old saxophone player on the Via Arenula. A fair exchange—talent for talent. And now this matchless gift to a pitiable hag.

Two days later, two blocks away, I cross the Via Vitorio Emanuelle in a mob of pedestrians which parts on the opposite sidewalk like water to reveal—life after death. A miracle. There stands in pure repose, a cigarette poised on her extended fingers, my trembling beggar. Healed. On break. Intermission. She's a dance stylist, that is, if she's a woman. A performance art graduate of the Rome Beggars' Conservatory. I want to shake her steady hand, ask for her autograph.

"Can you not go home to Nicaragua?" Cyndi asks, her voice all kindness. Why isn't she afraid? From where does this love come? She loves this poor man, this emblem of Central America, who wishes he could work for the grubby wages of American agri-business.

"I lost my passport. Help me, please." A face of abject loss and sorrow. Why is he this way? I can't discern the artful performance in his manner. I have seen this face, but I do not know this face. I have not known life without possibility, in which, despite despair and exhaustion, you walk up to strangers and, expecting to be brushed away, ask them to save you with a little money so that you can go one more day, sleep one more alley night on hard ground. Gnats, flies, and beggars.

I turn away again to count out three thousand colones—six American dollars. He takes the money, thanks us, and crosses the street to the restaurant counter, where we see him take away a paper plate of pizza, the sides squared up like stingray fins. He walks away quickly, hungrily, toward the dark, deserted corner, where he disappears.

Now we can resume our annoyed, impatient vigil for the rental car from San José, nearly two hours late. Problems of the known world, trivially real.

The next day, a man on the beach in Matapalo, in long pants and a plaid shirt, wears the same mask of suffering, approaches, stops ten feet from us, an unthreatening distance, and speaks Spanish.

"Hola. Buenos días. Quieren comprar algunas limones?" He shows us a plastic bag of small limes and one small pale, yellow mango. We buy.

He says, "Bye-bye." His father lost one leg in a car accident. Pantomimed. Steering. A sharp cutting gesture.

Rhosymedre in Cochran Chapel

In Guanacaste Province, the howler monkey roars like King Kong. On the verandah, Sally, a stray dog, chews on her colony of fleas. In this dry February, 2011, a tan midday breeze dusts through the bamboo.

Memory dusts as it does, synthesizing, fracturing, self-inventing. For a full week after the bell choir plays in Baltimore's University Baptist Church, the music rises again and again, music that's followed me for fifty-eight years. Its best visits come as preludes to the brief weekday services in Cochran Chapel. Lorene Banta, a fine organist, plays us into our assigned seats, a benign Mona Lisa smile, her hair pinned high on her head.

A gray dove bobs its Egyptian head along the stony path. A startled ctenosaur leaps from a tree and clunks onto the red, metal roof, under a few white clouds.

It's 1954, and in the white darkness of winter term, I slouch among the Vs in a back pew—Vance, Vander Ven, Van Raalte. Some instructor, maybe Simeon Hyde, checks off our perfunctory attendance. The hierarchy of prep school is ubiquitous. Even in the non-denominational democracy of chapel, we stand, sit, and bow by classes, lowers with lowers, uppers among uppers. Still, neither posturing with cigarettes nor smirking over dinner nor fixing the girls of Abbott with our hormonal gaze, we seem to find some common ground in those few ritual minutes. Pews with heads like hedges.

No rain in more than a month. The hibiscus hedge at latitude 10° north wears a heavy coat, dust of ATVs, SUVs, and basso profundo semis, rolling down the narrow road of dirt and rocks, north to Ostional or south to Samara. The oboeing and drumming of motorcycles.

In the course of two years at Andover, rich with performances of *The Mikado*, *The Student Prince*, and the *Fauré Requiem*, whether Dr. Banta plays "Rhosymedre" one time or nine times, for me it is this music in Cochran Chapel that most endures, deepened across the decades in other cities on various FM stations. And now a simple Google accesses plenty of YouTube permutations—from pipe organs to high school bands, though they sound pretty tinny, overwhelmed by the profound reverberation in my brain of Cochran's first organ, a Casavant.

"Rhosymedre's" lyrical, meditative voices gave consolation then and give it now amid the losses of age more than a half-century later. Composed by Ralph Vaughan Williams thirty years before I first heard it on a vinyl LP in the early '50s, this variation on J. D. Edwards' hymn-song of nearly 200 years ago, has a meekness not found in the portentous immensity of, say, Samuel Barber's "Adagio for Strings." It is a Möbius strip of music without coda that suspends in loops of sound like the prayer in T. S. Eliot's "Ash Wednesday"—"Teach us to sit still. "Rhosymedre" ends in its beginning.

But maybe this is wishful memory, my chapel version of an older colleague's reverence for "Red Sails in the Sunset." I see that I want to have it both ways, averring significance and apologizing for sentimentality, something like the narrator of Philip Larkin's "Church Going," who bicycles through the English countryside, stopping at an abandoned church: "Hatless, I take off / my cycle clips in awkward reverence." Of Cochran Chapel, Larkin would say, setting aside the shuffling and sweating of young men always ambitious for the next moment—the Wednesday game, the newspaper deadline, or the admissions acceptance—that it is "a serious house on serious ground." In its space we may have cosmic glimpses and hints of our own character. The beautiful mathematics of aging melody spiral amid the tall oak columns.

Meanwhile, dozing beneath the foot pedals and soaring above a high trumpet organ stop lie our entangled, unsounding beliefs. Generously, no one asks. No one has to controvert anything. We sing of saints "who from their labors rest," and then we run like seven-year-olds to the commons to be first in line for dinner and maybe steal an extra piece of cake. I try once and am caught.

A Black-headed Trogon, with its erotically brilliant yellow breast, perches on a branch in the dusty wind of the road to Ostional. The bird seems poised to say something, a sentient word about survival, post-Darwinian and witty. More aware and ironic about the planet than we.

We are secular, we are a heterodox flock, we are old believers. Among the Episcopalians, Unitarians, Catholics, and Jews stand erstwhile Methodists, renegade Lutherans, brash atheists, groping agnostics—diverse fugitives from the faith of our parents. Pastor A. Graham Baldwin presides over our services, but not over our spiritual pilgrimages. Not that I can infer. In hymns, we vow a kind of imminent, general dedication: "Once to every man and nation comes the moment to decide. . . ."

Gray undersides grow on these tropical clouds. A Tico tries with a machete to dislodge from a barbed-wire fence an animal with a prehensile tail and greenish quills on its head, maybe a porcupossum. What are their intentions?

And where is the Emperor of Ice Cream when we need him? Wallace Stevens dies unnoticed the year we matriculate. Robert Frost dies like grandpa of natural causes in 1963. Someone writes contemptuously that Frost articulates "the last sweepings of the Puritan latrine." Meanwhile, in our inscrutable evanescence, we lose ourselves in graduate school, law school, submarine school, Wall Street.

Of the more than two hundred species of mammals in Costa Rica, half are bats, vacuuming up at dusk the country's illimitable squadrons of flying insects. By day they hang under our dark eaves and chirp like smoke detectors.

Are we diminished by the possibility that the universe does not watch over us? Belief empowers, but it can still be illusional. The brain is wider than the sky. And the sky is wider than the brain. We creep along a paradox of consciousness. Is all this capability a gift so that we can communicate with divinity? Or is it a way to choose whether to understand the world as divinely ordered for our possible comprehension and even our salvation? And possibly to recognize our profound finitude? The brain's billion neurons labor to comprehend immensities, and they also imagine—vividly and persuasively—immensities that are not.

A grasshopper the size of a bratwurst crawls along a yellow-flowered vine. The ctenosaur eats its blossoms.

I don't know how it is that the dark beauty and luminous sorrow of music soar above this daze. My friend and colleague of many decades, Lester Wolfson, still declares in his 88th year that his faith in our potential to learn and to love is best expressed by great music—of Mozart, Puccini, Chopin. Music and the music of language strangely circumscribe the terror of the Dakota grasslands, the swells of the Pacific, and the galaxies. But the wild birds along the roads of this rich coast—from Samara to Santa Marta to San Juanillo—sing with bearable immediacy. In that way, perhaps, Cochran Chapel and "Rhosymedre" prelude our capacity for the music of stillness.

Now Like a Dream

January 13, 1885. At her writing table in the parlor of the Colfax house in South Bend, ELLEN COLFAX *pauses to read the letter she is writing.*

ELLEN   January 13, 1885. Dear Carrie. In the midst of what has happened, I reach out to you. I cannot say why. This solitude is stolen. I belong to his public now and for days to come. Peter Studebaker has just called—to tell me what soon the whole country will know, and you, long before this one letter reaches you in the West. He asked me questions. Had I heard from Schuyler? Was he in Mankato this morning? And then, "A stranger is said to have dropped dead there in the depot this morning." And I knew. He wanted me to say it for him. So I did. The winter grows bitter. More snow comes. Oh, yes, I can say why I write to you first. I see us all in Colorado. At South Park. On Mt. Lincoln. Nearly seventeen years gone by. The mountain sky was blue, blue—so far—

SCHUYLER   (*Appearing in the doorway.*) Nellie. (*Startled, as if from a trance,* ELLEN *looks around, composes herself, and covers her letter with a book. He goes to her, kisses her cheek and turns away, interested in a book he carries. He paces a little and then turns back to her.*) Are you all right?

ELLEN   Why, yes. I was writing to Carrie.

SCHUYLER   You seem troubled.

ELLEN   (*Going to him and putting her hand on his forehead.*) You promised me you would rest in the library.

SCHUYLER   I hadn't thought I was confined. Here is the most wonderful book. The language puzzles me at times. It is not a polite book. But this man. I wonder that I don't know him. He was in Washington during the war. I could have passed him on the street. And now we're here in Indiana, done with Washington for good. How long home? A month? And I discover him here in the library.

ELLEN   Who are you talking about?

SCHUYLER   Let me read something to you. "The Four Years' War is over—and in the peaceful, strong, exciting, fresh occasions of Today, and of the Future, that strange, sad war is hurrying even now to be forgotten. The camp, the drill, the liens of sentries, the prisons, the hospitals—(ah! The hospitals!)—all have passed away—all seem now like a dream. A new race, a young and lusty generation, already sweeps in with ocean currents, obliterating war, and all its scars, its mounded graves"—

ELLEN   Stop! I'm sorry, dear. Please. Go on. And tell me who this is.

SCHUYLER   "So let it be obliterated. I say the life of the present and the future makes undeniable demands upon us each and all, South, North, East, West . . . . To help put the United States (even if only in imagination) hand in hand, in one unbroken circle in a chant"—

ELLEN   (*Covering the page with her hand, then taking the book.*) *Leaves of Grass.* Why are you so moved by this . . . . what is this writing?

SCHUYLER   It's a kind of poetry. What I hear in it brings the war years back vividly, out of a dream.

ELLEN   A dreadful dream. After eight years, we deserve to sleep in peace.

SCHUYLER   Yes, I know. And after eighteen years in Washington, my thoughts should be home here in South Bend. I should be resting. But I'm not dead, Nellie. (*She turns away, unnoticed, her face in her hands.*) And the war is still alive and will live on—in the reasons for which we fought. There remains yet so much to be done.

ELLEN   Can't you leave the work to those in office?

SCHUYLER   Well, of course, I must. My power and influence have passed with the election. But the waters of the mind flow on, don't you know?

ELLEN   Yes, but the body doesn't flow so fast as once it did. Come and sit down. These leaves of grass will go on growing. You forget your illness, Schuyler. (*Leading him to a chair.*)

SCHUYLER   You don't. And that was two years ago.

ELLEN   You might have died.

SCHUYLER   But I didn't. Instead, I gave up cigars. In return for which the doctor gave me twenty more years to live.

ELLEN   Which you propose to spend in the past. Think of us. Think of your son.

SCHUYLER   The path of the future begins in the past. It was a fearful and a wonderful thing that they did.

ELLEN   What thing?

SCHUYLER   The war to restore the union. They gave so much.

ELLEN   Sometimes I don't think you realize how much you gave.

SCHUYLER   I could never give enough. Beside those others. The thousands and thousands lost. The thousands shot, drowned in fast rivers, burned in the forest battle fires, wasted by disease in the prison pens. And the hospitals.

ELLEN   Schuyler.

SCHUYLER   (*Reading.*) "Ah! the hospitals!"

ELLEN   I'm going to finish my letter. (*Sitting at her table to write and struggling to ignore him.*) You go on reading your book of sorrow.

SCHUYLER   I know as surely as ever that the prize is worth it all. (*Thinking.*) This man I might have met in the woeful hospitals of Washington. Let me read you one more thing:

> From the stump of the arm, the amputated hand
> I undo the clotted lint, remove the slough, wash off the
>   matter and blood, ...
> I dress the wound in the side, deep, deep,
> But a day or two more, for see the frame all wasted and
>   sinking, ...
> Thus in silence in dreams' projections,
> Returning, resuming, I thread my way through the hospitals. . . .

I ought to have done more.

ELLEN   You visited in the hospitals, and no one ever worked harder than you did as Speaker of the House. And what about the legislation you sponsored, so that letters from soldiers would be paid for by those to whom they wrote? You did what you could.

SCHUYLER   It was so small a thing. We can never do enough. War asks us to give all. It is the deadliest scourge of mankind. War is the empty sleeve and the weary crutch. It is the wives and the children waiting.

ELLEN   And the children fighting. And dying under the colors. Was it worth such losses? The killing and mutilation of hundred of thousands of humans, many of them boys, still children? Can anything ever be worth such slaughter?

SCHUYLER   When you ask me that, Nellie, I cannot answer.

ELLEN   Imagine our little son, bearing your name, in just a dozen years, marching away to cruel battle and disease. Could you give him up?

SCHUYLER   (*Going to her and taking her hand.*) I understand what you say. One life, even one, is too dear a price to pay, and yet belief drove us to war with ourselves. The life blood of the Republic, the very air itself, free and for all people, was at issue. You know, it seems sometimes to me that nearly my whole life is public service, as an editor, as a representative in Congress, as its speaker, and finally as the nation's vice president, has somehow been tied to the original principle of the nation. Years before the war, fighting for the sovereignty of the people of the Kansas Territory, fighting to stop the corruption of slavery from spreading to the new territories and states. And then the war itself, the four long years looking into the contemptible face of secession, the endless, at times hopeless, destruction that we in office had to pursue so relentlessly. I don't mean to praise or pity myself. Forgive me. I was not a soldier. What I mean to say is that after the war the struggle to salvage the war's meaning went on. We had to make the country whole again. Oh, it is all there in the original text.

ELLEN   The original text?

SCHUYLER   The constitution. The fight wages on for what is already written. Why, remember last year, already seven years after the last cannon fell silent, the tie-breaking vote that I cast for the amendment to the general amnesty bill? When will this matter ever be resolved? If orderly, sober citizens of the United States cannot obtain food and lodging at public hotels like the rest of mankind, or even average accommodations of railroad trains after paying first-class fares, we should either acknowledge that the constitution is a nullity or insist on obedience to it by all, and protection under it for all. And do you remember that that amendment on equal rights was removed before the amnesty bill could pass? Our work is not finished. Well. I ought not to smother you with oratory. Forgive me.

ELLEN   It's been your special gift. It's what you've given to the country.

SCHUYLER   As for that, I'm out of office.

ELLEN   I suspect your speaking career will go on forever.

SCHUYLER   Only till I die, Nellie, and even then—

ELLEN   Please don't say such things.

SCHUYLER   But it's true. You know it is. Of course, I could lose my voice. There were election canvasses when I had to wrap my throat at night in damp cloths to recover my voice for the next day's speeches.

ELLEN   I think there will always be the next day's speeches.

SCHUYLER   Well, you have to allow me one vice, or at least one excess. In my youth I took the vow of temperance. The doctor forbids me to smoke. Maybe I'll just talk myself to death.

ELLEN   You don't know what you're saying. (*She sits at the table, her head bowed in sadness.*)

SCHUYLER   I confess to bewilderment, Nellie. I don't know when I've seen you so distressed. From the moment I came into the parlor there's been something under all your words. You seem afraid. Or sad.

ELLEN   Oh, I'm all right. I have my moods.

SCHUYLER   It's not like you to brood this way. Has something happened? (*ELLEN goes to him and holds him in a long embrace.*) I'll tell you what. You go back to your letter to Carrie. Write her all the news, such as it is. I'm going to read some more of these "drumtaps," and I won't make a sound. You'll think I'm resting. (*He sits and begins to read.* ELLEN *watches him for a moment and then returns to her letter.*)

ELLEN   (*Writing.*) He's here with me now, still alive and full of the nation's business. In my mind, for some reason, it's 1873. When I returned to life in South Bend, I suppose I didn't guess how much at heart he would always be a traveler and a speaker—even to the last cold morning in a railway station in Minnesota. How much he belonged among the people, always somehow able to feel with them.

SCHUYLER   (*Reading.*)
> A sight in camp in the daybreak gray and dim, . . .
> As slow I walk in the cool fresh air the path near by the
> hospital tent,
> Three forms I see on stretchers lying, brought out there
> untended lying,
> Over each the blanket spread, ample brownish woolen blanket,
> Gray and heavy blanket, folding, covering all.

ELLEN   (*Reading.*) "I think I must have missed the signs that he was failing this winter. Or he hid them from me. When I look back, I can see. He was so tired. Something drove him. It always did. How else explain his power to endure? No man ever had a stronger sense of duty. But there was something more. Something unfinished. Old business. I think I know."

SCHUYLER   (*Reading.*)
> Curious I halt and silent stand,
> Then with light fingers I from the face of the nearest the first
> just lift the blanket;
> Who are you elderly man so gaunt and grim, with well-gray'd
> hair,

And flesh all sunken about the eyes?
Who are you my dear comrade?
Then to the second I step—and who are you my child and
    darling?
Who are you sweet boy with cheeks yet blooming?

ELLEN   (*Writing.*) Could I have kept him home? For what? I would
have had to lock him in the library. And he would have been less
alive than now. Today he is gone from me but with me still.

SCHUYLER   (*Reading.*)

Then to the third—a face nor child nor old, very calm, as of
    beautiful yellow-white ivory;
Young man I think I know you—I think this is the face of
    The Christ himself.
Dead and divine and brother of all, and here again he lies.
(*Pauses.*) What will the people of the world think of me when
    someday they pass my coffin?

ELLEN   I think he is with God—in whom he rests. Tired no more.

SCHUYLER   Nellie. (*Setting the book aside.*)

ELLEN   Are you through reading?

SCHUYLER   I need to talk to you about something that weighs on
my mind much of the time, and, while I don't know how to ease
the burden, I need to talk. It would help me to know that you
understand.

ELLEN   You don't need to explain anything.

SCHUYLER   (*Rising and pacing.*) I fear we will never find the man
to whom Oakes Ames gave $1,200. I fear that I will never be
able to provide documented, conclusive evidence that I never
received Crédit Mobilier stocks, nor even a penny of dividends.
God knows my innocence, and I believe that you know it. But
after all the damage done by the newspapers, how will history
judge me? Ames's unreliable story disappeared. As did the man
that Mr. Dillon saw receive the money Ames claimed to have
given me. As if I would risk dealing with so suspect a corpora-
tion as Crédit Mobilier. This scandal has fallen full across the

face of my career. I am in eclipse.

ELLEN   The light of your public service will shine again.

SCHUYLER   When I learned the Crédit Mobilier was under attack in court, I told Ames I didn't want the stock. And I never received it.

ELLEN   The people trust you.

SCHUYLER   Do they? Do they believe my innocence? Or do they forgive me? These questions haunt me. Not so much for me. Man is nothing. But his principles are everything. My life work has been a public trust. Is it now to be nullified because of an unsubstantiated accusation by an unreliable man and by the human hunger for any bad news?

ELLEN   The people have always trusted you. Now trust them. They know you.

SCHUYLER   As if it were immoral for a public officer to purchase stock in the Crédit Mobilier, or the Crédit Immobilier, if there is one, or in the Union Pacific, or Central Pacific, or Northern Pacific, or Southern Pacific. Never have my actions in office been influenced by my personal financial interests in any business on earth. I am not a corrupt man.

ELLEN   If only when the issue first became public, you had given a full account of the terms of your purchase. They thought you were hiding when you had nothing to hide.

SCHUYLER   Yes, Nellie, I know that I made mistakes. The allegations stunned me at first. I am not yet recovered, but somehow I will find a way to reaffirm my life's work and to recover the public's trust. Do you think I can?

ELLEN   I think you have to let the issue run its course. The newspapers will find other news. The Crédit Mobilier is one small moment in a lifetime. And people forget.

SCHUYLER   Do I want people to forget?

ELLEN   Do you want the names Schuyler Colfax and Crédit Mobilier to be remembered together forever? I should think you would want the connection forgotten.

SCHUYLER   It is not forgetting that I want. It is vindication.

ELLEN   Will you conduct hearings? Will you need to explain your-
self? Let your eighteen years in Washington speak for you.

SCHUYLER   People forget. I think you said that.

ELLEN   Come here and sit down. Even you can forget.

SCHUYLER   Never, Nellie. Never.

ELLEN   (*Leading him to his chair where she makes him sit, as if a child
or an invalid, and she stands behind him, gently stroking his forehead.*)
Close your eyes.

SCHUYLER   I see better in the dark.

ELLEN   You're such a stubborn thing. You persist.

SCHUYLER   I count persistence as a virtue.

ELLEN   Well, I can count it, too.

SCHUYLER   Four years have taught me that. I concede persistence
to you and admire it.

ELLEN   Match your admiration with obedience. And silence, too. I
want to tell you something. A little while ago you thought I was
preoccupied.

SCHUYLER   You were troubled and—

ELLEN   Shhhhh! You're forbidden. I was not troubled. I was simply
somewhere else. And you were, too. In fact, in August it will be
five years since the great Colorado Territory expedition of 1868.
A certain distinguished Speaker of the House and future Vice
President, with a well-appointed retinue and a virtual harem of
young and charming and—

SCHUYLER   Persistent—

ELLEN   —handsome ladies, journeyed by railway car, part of the
way in the car that had been President Lincoln's, and by stage
across the plains and into the mountain wilderness of the West,
seeking at great peril of their lives to civilize a rude and heathen
people.

SCHUYLER   They were sightseers.

ELLEN   They were missionaries. (*Putting her hand over his mouth.*)
Once a Speaker of the House, always a Speaker of the House.

To resume the story, sir, on the twenty-four-hour stagecoach ride from Cheyenne down to Denver, only the charm and diplomacy of the future Vice President, an Easterner—from South Bend— saved the party from starvation. His persuasion won a frontier breakfast for them from a cross and recalcitrant station master's wife. (*Sighs.*) Our hero. But harder times were ahead. And great deeds of heroism. The children of the Great Father traveled high into the Rocky Mountains, into a region where Arapahoe Indians were at that very moment killing settlers. There in South Park, far from Denver mansions, Indians blocked their way. The wagons were drawn in a circle. The women were terrified of being kid- napped, but no less a hero than the honorable Schuyler Colfax guaranteed their safety from the Indians. He bravely exclaimed, "If the Indians attack, I'm going to shoot the girls." But the women were not afraid. Just as bravely, they replied, "We would rather take our chances with the Indians."

SCHUYLER   You knew I didn't know how to shoot a gun.

ELLEN   With Indians coming, that fact was not reassuring.

SCHUYLER   They were friendly Utes. We smoked a pipe of peace. Now I'm not allowed to smoke.

ELLEN   I'm glad we women didn't have to put that dirty old pipe in our mouths.

SCHUYLER   And you were jealous of Sue Matthews because Chief Washington wanted to buy her.

ELLEN   Well, he offered four horses for her.

SCHUYLER   (*Rising and going to her.*) If he had had more horses, he would have offered to buy you.

ELLEN   A peculiar flattery.

SCHUYLER   He told me so. That was when I realized your worth and vowed to propose to you. Our engagement on that trip was what finally civilized the territory, after I had been trying to tame it in Congress for ten years.

ELLEN   You love the West, don't you?

SCHUYLER   I do believe that if the frontier had been more developed in 1836, when my family migrated from New York to New Carlisle, we might have gone on to Colorado. I was thirteen then, and there were Indians hunting in the woods of Northern Indiana. There were deer feeding in herds, and bears prowled about. But that was nearly forty years ago. And now the railroads are tying the coasts together from east to west.

ELLEN   You're feeling better.

SCHUYLER   (*He takes her hand and touches her wedding band.*) Here is our Colorado gold, sent to me by a miner who washed it out of the mountains for you, when he heard of our engagement. I want to travel again, Nellie. I've had more requests to speak. They seem to come from everywhere. Minnesota, Iowa, Illinois. There will be an unveiling of a statue of Lincoln in Springfield in the fall. We'll go together and share that event.

ELLEN   President Lincoln would have wanted you there.

SCHUYLER   I think I have some things to say to the people on his behalf.

ELLEN   (*Sitting at her table.*) I guess you have a speech or two on Lincoln in you. No one knows his presidency better.

SCHUYLER   He kept the country whole, and he brought the people back together. We need to understand that.

ELLEN   You still have work to do.

SCHUYLER   If I can just talk to America. And if it will listen to me. And believe me. All my life, it seems, no matter how hard and how long the road before me lies, there is a never-sleeping something in me that whispers, "Go on! Go on!"

ELLEN   (*Writing.*) Remember the dream I had in Colorado, Carrie? I dreamed that you and I were sleeping in an upper window of an old and very high mill. A clear and beautiful stream of water flowed by, and we were admiring the flashes of sunlight upon it, when all at once you glanced down at a plot of grass between the river and the mill, and exclaimed, "Oh, Nellie, I see my old precious ring down there!" and immediately started for it. When you got down, you stooped and picked it up and put it on your finger.

It was an opal. And very beautiful. There were some other rings lying on the grass, and you said, carelessly, to me, "Get you one, too, Nellie!" Wasn't it strange?

CURTAIN

Akira Hashiguchi

The Vandalia Cat Murders

HAROLD DOBSON, 70, a retired banker.
MARGARET DOBSON, 70, a woman devoted to cats.

Vandalia, a rural town in Iowa, in the year 2002.
Act I: *Noon, evening, and the following morning.*
Scene 1: *A weekday noon in May.*
MARGARET is preparing lunch as HAROLD enters the kitchen from the back porch, setting his briefcase by the door. He wears a suit, even in warm weather, though he will take it off and roll up his sleeves when he's at home. MARGARET usually wears a kind of smock around the house with large, practical pockets. From time to time she takes from one of the pockets a small journal in which she writes notes to herself.

MARGARET   (*Without looking up from the counter.*) It's nearly ready. Coffee with or after?

HAROLD   (*Entering the half-bath off the kitchen.*) After, please.

MARGARET   (*Singing.*) "What'll I do when you are far away, and I am blue—"

HAROLD   Did the mail come?

MARGARET   "What'll I do with just a photograph to tell my troubles to—"

HAROLD   (*Coming out of the bathroom.*) Did the mail come?

MARGARET   Nothing of interest.

HAROLD   (*Sitting at the table and tucking a napkin into his collar.*) By the way, Charlie Hoyt broke his hip, and Esther says he's going to spend some time in a nursing home. I need you to go visit him for me.

MARGARET   I'll go with you.

HAROLD   We've gone around on this before. I can't do it.

MARGARET   I'll be right there with you.

HAROLD   I can't go into those places. It's like looking down into the grave.

MARGARET   Well, imagine how they must feel.

HAROLD   I tried stopping by on my way home, and I couldn't do it.

MARGARET   What happened?

HAROLD   I got nauseated. People near death have an odor.

MARGARET   I can't say that I look forward to those visits either. There's a kind of hush over age and illness. The waiting.

HAROLD   I don't want to talk about this anymore.

MARGARET   It's supposed to be good to talk through these things.

HAROLD   I get things in my head that won't go away.

MARGARET   What things?

HAROLD   The smell of cat pee in the yard is getting worse.

MARGARET   It's the junipers. I never liked them.

HAROLD   It's not the junipers. But let's enjoy our lunch.

MARGARET   (*Bringing a bowl of salad to the table.*) There's avocado in this, but you can pick it out.

HAROLD   Do we have any T'ousand Island?

MARGARET   (*Handing him a bottle and buttoning his shirt.*) You missed a button on your shirt this morning.

HAROLD   What's the point of avocado?

MARGARET   (*Sitting down at the table.*) I think the point of avocado is avocado. It just wants to be an avocado. That's all it asks. Do you like the bread?

HAROLD   It looks like mice got into the flour.

MARGARET   You don't have to eat it.

HAROLD   I'm sorry, Mother. You fixed a nice lunch.

MARGARET   You don't have to eat it.

HAROLD   Simple, whole-wheat bread. One color. One grain.

MARGARET   For a simple, whole-wheat life.

HAROLD   It's a good life, Mother. And you know what? We worked hard for it. Vandalia isn't one of the Seven Wonders. We know that. Still, it's a nice place to live—

MARGARET   —but I wouldn't want to visit here. As you always say. (*She reaches for a brochure on top of a pile of pamphlets and shows him a picture.*) Speaking of places to visit, can you just imagine what it would be like to stand at the summit of this path, 7,000 feet above the sea, where ancient people lived amid the clouds and their gods?

HAROLD   They're all dead and so is their civilization. Does that tell you anything about their gods? The sparks fly upward.

MARGARET   People die, Harold.

HAROLD   And so would we, trying to climb up there.

MARGARET   We'd just have to take our time.

HAROLD   Mother, at our age we've got no business climbing around in the Andes.

MARGARET   I already have. (*She touches a finger to her head.*)

HAROLD   (*Pointing to his head.*) What's this about? Your disappearances?

MARGARET   Harold, we have an understanding.

HAROLD   Just checking. Making sure.

MARGARET   Look here. We really could manage this trip. Two weeks at sea level.

HAROLD   Oh, for God's sake! Darwin!

MARGARET   The Galapagos Islands! Imagine walking in his footsteps.

HAROLD   By the end of the first week you'll have pet names for every bird and turtle.

MARGARET   Darwin already named them.

HAROLD   Fluffy and Pouncer?

MARGARET   What can I do to get you to take a trip with me?

HAROLD   It's the places you come up with. Finland. Kurdistan. Those Indian Ocean islands. Look at these places. (*Holds up brochures.*)

MARGARET   Yes, look at them.

HAROLD   Why not Las Vegas? Why not Branson?

MARGARET   With your Rotary Club cronies.

HAROLD   My "cronies," as you like to call them, are fine men. And you know what? They're successful men with fine wives. Salt of the earth.

MARGARET   Las Vegas is not salt of the earth.

HAROLD   (*Throwing down the brochures, taking off his napkin, and rising.*) We're not going to talk about this. It's a waste of time. We're not going to fly off to Spain and have some Islamic fanatics blow us up in midair.

MARGARET   Do you want coffee?

HAROLD   I want a nap. (*Leaving the kitchen, he drops her travel literature in the waste can.*) A complete waste. (*After he leaves, she recovers her brochures, puts them on the shelf above the kitchen desk, and begins clearing the table, as HAROLD returns.*) Now, then. Back to the bank. Collinsworth's trying to jew me down on an interest rate. (*MARGARET turns to look at him briefly, but says nothing.*) You're upset with me, Mother?

MARGARET   I have asked you repeatedly not to use that expression.

HAROLD   It's just a saying. Collinsworth's not even a Jew.

MARGARET   It's not just a saying.

HAROLD   He's trying to Muslim me down. He's trying to Mexican me down. Take your pick. You're upset with me.

MARGARET   I'm upset with you?

HAROLD   Yes, you're upset with me. You're on edge these days.

MARGARET   I'm on edge?

HAROLD   And please don't repeat my words.

MARGARET   What response would you expect from such accusatory questions?

HAROLD   (*Opening the door to the porch.*) You're upset with me.

MARGARET   Everything upsets you. The bread, talk about travel, and avocados, of all things! Ask yourself what's the matter.

HAROLD   Can you smell the cat pee?

MARGARET   They have kidneys. Bladders, too. Sally's picking me up in the morning. I'm going to spend a few days with her. I'm going to talk to her about a trip.

HAROLD   (*Closing the door, walking over to the desk and shuffling through a pile.*) I don't want to talk anymore about trips. Where's today's mail?

MARGARET   It's very lonely talking to myself.

HAROLD   Why are we getting mail from the Un-American Civil Liberties Union? Are you sending them money?

MARGARET   I cancelled your membership. They keep asking you to renew.

HAROLD   That isn't funny.

MARGARET   It isn't funny.

HAROLD   We built this country so that people can stand up on their own hind legs and make a go of it. We've got resources. We've got education for everyone, we've got laws, and we've got a constitution that guarantees everyone a fair chance. But having provided all that, we've got to step aside and let the market play out the game, let people compete—the immigrants, all those Mexicans, the legal ones, after we zip up the borders—let 'em rise and fall on their own ability and their willingness to do a full day's work and some overtime. Instead, we've turned the country into a continental day care center for the wishful thinkers, the lazy, the complacent, and—the—the—the unfaithful.

MARGARET   Who are the unfaithful? What do you mean—

HAROLD   The unbelievers, the weak-kneed doubters who spend all their time making excuses. Their parents neglected them. I guess I know a little about that. And their schools that didn't teach them. Some of us had to teach ourselves. They were poor, they were sick, they were victims of one thing or another—just excuses for lying down in the road where men with gumption run over them on their way to work. The liberals with their handouts and the ACLU with their namby-pamby hand-holding. Hands off! That's the rule we've turned our backs on. Hands off! It worked for me. And you know what? Nobody gave me anything.

MARGARET   That's not exactly true, Harold.

HAROLD   It damned well is true. Where were my parents? All I had was myself and my God-given willingness to roll up my sleeves and get the job done. In the sweat of our brows we toil.

MARGARET   You had a family. You had Ida Grove.

HAROLD   Ida Grove! People took me in because they saw something in me.

MARGARET   If I'm not mistaken, you were only two years old.

HAROLD   Why do you belittle me? Why do you minimize what I worked for my entire life?

MARGARET   You worked very hard. You were a good provider.

HAROLD   I took over the bank when it was a storefront with a shoe box for a vault. I foreclosed on some of the poorest-run farms in southwestern Iowa, and I made them turn a profit.

MARGARET   And, as I recall, on the seventh day, you rested.

HAROLD   Don't mock me, Margaret. Don't talk that way. You're part of all this. We built an empire and we sold it for a fortune.

MARGARET   I built nothing. I fixed your meals. I starched your shirts. I still starch your shirts, but I don't know why. Every day you go to your office at the bank, but for what?

HAROLD   Now, then, there's questions at the bank no one else can answer. There's forty years of financial history in this head. I am the bank.

MARGARET   You were the bank.

HAROLD   I will always be the bank.

MARGARET   And if you die tomorrow, the bank dies.

HAROLD   You know what I mean.

MARGARET   No, I don't. You're retired. You don't have a job any-more. You could sit at your desk at the bank and take up knitting. You could stay home and wander around the house in your slip-pers. You could leave town. You could sail around the world. You could soak in the thermals baths of Iceland.

HAROLD   The solution to all problems. (*Opening the door again to leave.*) Take a vacation. Take a trip. Disappear. Why is that?

MARGARET   I've never said it was a solution to anything.

HAROLD   You've done it often enough. (*She ignores him.*) Do you smell that? It's cats. (*Closes the door again.*) And where are the birds? The feeders are still full. Where are the squirrels?

MARGARET   I'm not a census taker.

HAROLD   You said there was no mail.

MARGARET   Nothing of interest. What are you looking for?

HAROLD   I have people checking on some background for me.

MARGARET   What are you talking about?

HAROLD   You know there's no need to talk about this. There's noth-ing to talk about.

MARGARET   There certainly seems to be something important to ask about.

HAROLD   It's nothing that should concern you.

MARGARET   I know what you're doing, Harold. I know what this is about. This isn't the first time.

HAROLD   Does a marble know why it's rolling around on a checker board? A man needs to know who he is, but does he know why he needs to know? The Jews have their history. They've got their identity. But you know what? For all their sins, and God knows they're a cursed people, they know their place in history, and when you know your story, you understand what you were chosen for. All this striving isn't just aimless. It's not pinball. We have our destinies. Does this make any sense to you, Margaret?

MARGARET   I don't know what "know" means. But if you think it will somehow help you to find out who your parents are, then I guess you have to do it.

HAROLD   I need to know my name, and it isn't Harold Dobson.

MARGARET   Names are only names. I took your name forty-nine years ago. Was I somebody else before I was Margaret Dobson?

HAROLD   Tour your travel books. (*Opens the door to the porch again.*) Get out your National Geographics. Daub yourself with clay or stick bone splinters through your ear lobes.

MARGARET   You only make yourself ridiculous when you talk like that.

HAROLD   (*As he starts to leave.*) This pee smell. How can you stand it? I counted five cats in the old maple tree this morning.

MARGARET   Only five?

HAROLD   Before the neighborhood's overrun, you better call county animal control.

MARGARET   Sally is picking me up tomorrow morning, and I'll be gone till Thursday.

HAROLD   Two nights. Why do you have to be away so long?

MARGARET   Two nights with our daughter needs an explanation?

HAROLD   At least I'd know where you are. While you're at it, find out why she won't speak to me. Never mind. Don't make her think it matters.

MARGARET　It ought to matter. You ought to care what she thinks about you.

HAROLD　Do I not pay her bills? (*He leaves.* MARGARET *watches through the window to see that he has left, and then she brings out many cans of cat food, opens them, and spoons the food into dishes as she looks out the window to the side yard.*)

MARGARET　Oh, you're so hungry! Poor mommas and babies. I should have fed you hours and hours ago. I am so, so sorry. Here comes a bowl for the calicos. And a bowl for the tigers. Wait your turn, Samantha. There's plenty for everyone. And here's for the tabbies. Esmerada, you have to keep strong to feed the new litter. And now the gray-eyed cats. And the black cats. The seven black cats of the night. Cats with yellow eyes. Moon cats, their tails curled together in a great wreath of cat fur, shining out of the trees and wrapping themselves around the moon. (*She places the dishes on a large tray and carries the tray out onto the porch.*)

END OF SCENE

Act I, Scene 2: The same day.
Through the kitchen window, darkness falls. MARGARET *is sitting at the kitchen table, drinking coffee and reading.*

HAROLD　(*Returning from his weekly meeting of professional men, apparently agitated.*) Why are you sitting here, Mother? We have a houseful of recliners and rockers and ottomans, and here you sit at the kitchen table.

MARGARET　This is my favorite room.

HAROLD　We can move a bed in here. You'll never have to leave.

MARGARET　I don't live in this kitchen.

HAROLD　We can board it up. Or we'll rent out the rest of the house. Turn it into a hotel. A hotel for cats.

MARGARET　How was your Rotary Club tonight?

HAROLD　Nothing special.

MARGARET　Was everyone there? Was it a nice program?

HAROLD   If you're a big fan of the United Nations.

MARGARET   It is Rotary International.

HAROLD   This global inclusivity thing is thin ice. Now that all the Arabs want us dead, why do we still act like we're all friends? The world's divided into two camps. One of these days, when the U.N. comes apart at the seams, Rotary will look pretty silly. (*He walks into the pantry.*)

MARGARET   Can I get you anything? Are you still hungry?

HAROLD   No, I'm not hungry. I'm just browsing. (*He walks out of the pantry with a large, heavy box which he sets down hard on the kitchen counter and begins to look through the contents.*) When I got home, I counted eleven cats in the yard. Are you running a cat restaurant out of our kitchen?

MARGARET   Only eleven cats? It's getting dark. You can't have counted them all.

HAROLD   This morning there were five. How many are there?

MARGARET   Oh, well, I suppose there are more than eleven.

HAROLD   Why haven't I known about this? Why haven't I been kept informed?

MARGARET   Harold, you live here. There's no mystery.

HAROLD   There's secrecy. This afternoon I called Sherman at County Animal Control, and he said they'd already had complaints about the cats, but he said that when they came by, you told them the cats were your family and that they were well-cared for, and the county was not to interfere with a family matter. And you know what? Sherman acted surprised that I didn't know about it.

MARGARET   I'm not surprised.

HAROLD   Now, then. I want the yard back, Mother. We have a yard, not a stockyard. (*He begins taking cans out of the box and setting them on the counter noisily. She gets up from her chair at the table and begins to put the cans back into the box.*) I would prefer that you not interfere. (*He takes them back out.*) Can't you just taste all these flavors: Salmon, chicken, lamb, beef, fish. Let's dig down a little farther. Ah, here's bluegill! Perch. And, of course, our favorite. Catfish! Oh, and here come the birds! Canary and wren. What, no hummingbird! And no vegetables? Ah, wait, here they come. Zucchini, broccoli, asparagus. And pole beans. Pole beans for pole cats. Tell me, Mother, is this food for cats or for humans?

MARGARET   You're being foolish.

HAROLD   Maybe these flavors appeal to little old ladies in Iowa with nothing to do, with time on their hands. So, why not, let's tamper with the natural order of things. Let's open a soup kitchen. Or set up a hog trough. We can just haul a bucket of cat food out to slop the cats. We'll have cat-calling at the county fair. Best of show for the brood tabby. We'll soon be dealing in cat futures.

MARGARET   Everything I do you find a way to make ridiculous.

HAROLD   (*Holding up many cans of cat food.*) This is, in itself, ridiculous.

MARGARET   You don't know what you're talking about. These are beautiful creatures with a rightful place in the world.

HAROLD   Rightful? Tell me about rightful. Why do cats exist? Do these yard cats have a niche in the eco-system? They don't hunt. They don't hunt for you, and they certainly don't have to hunt for themselves now that they belong to an eating club.

MARGARET   You wouldn't know this, but left to themselves, they have a devastating effect on the bird population.

HAROLD   You can't eat them, you can't ride them. Security? Did Si the junkman have a junkyard cat? They don't do tricks. You can't even teach them to sit up. Or bring in the paper. Do they know their own names? I'm pretty sure that "Here, Kitty" works for every cat on the planet if you've got a bowl of food in your hand. I do not understand why you are doing this.

MARGARET   Do you have to understand everything? Can I not be allowed some part of the world that isn't under your supervision? Do you have to disparage these poor creatures that do no harm to you? You're filled with some sort of anger toward a species that's not like you. It's—it's like bigotry.

HAROLD   Fine! Report me to the Anti-Defamation League. By the way, what are the constitutional rights of cats?

MARGARET   You think because you're so smart or rich that you can do anything you want with other creatures.

HAROLD   God gave man dominion over all the creatures of the earth. All I'm talking about is dominion over the yard.

MARGARET   What are you proposing to do?

HAROLD   To begin, you're not to feed these cats anymore.

MARGARET   And if I don't agree to that?

HAROLD   Then I'll remove them myself.

MARGARET   That I would like to see. You rounding up cats.

HAROLD   I will not waste my time chasing cats around. But you know what? I will get rid of them. Do you understand me?

MARGARET   You have that look in your eye, like some sort of predator. I've seen it before.

HAROLD   Predator! That's silly.

MARGARET   You've made up your mind to do this, haven't you? You're of a mind to kill, and now all you need is an excuse, some kind of invented necessity. This is the starlings all over again.

HAROLD   Good grief, Margaret, not the starlings again.

MARGARET   I won't forget what a slaughter that was, your hunter friends all out there firing into the trees, and starlings, dead and dying, falling from the sky like a plague upon Pharoah. And the children from the neighborhood chasing after the wounded with sticks. What possesses you? It's as though from time to time you men need to start shooting at something. At anything. Just kill. I don't know where that comes from. Strip off your clothes and paint your face. Build a big fire and dance around it. Howl! Yowl!

HAROLD   The sparks fly upward. But I'm not a savage, Mother.

MARGARET   This is not about cats.

HAROLD   This is only about cats. It's about cat management. Don't try to turn this into some big idea.

MARGARET   Management! You're going to kill my cats. This is an execution.

HAROLD   Don't dignify these cats and all their fleas. This is not a firing squad with little blindfolds.

MARGARET   You know I don't like to make speeches. I'm not very good at it. But let me show you this. I know you think I'm crazy, that this is just some old lady's delusion, but here's a place called Cat Sanctuary where volunteers care for cats in a shelter. (*She shows him a brochure which he ignores.*) Hundreds of cats. And international volunteers. Abandoned cats have a home here where they get medical attention—spayed, neutered, vaccinated. This sanctuary has been on the Discovery Channel.

HAROLD   Where do you get your information? You sound like a fundraiser.

MARGARET   I'm fighting for these cats' lives.

HAROLD   Where is this place?

MARGARET   That doesn't matter.

HAROLD   Where is it?

MARGARET   Italy.

HAROLD   Eurocats. Great!

MARGARET   What is that supposed to mean?

HAROLD   Let's not get into European cat welfare. What Europeans do with European cats is their business. Not every animal has to live on the best of terms. Not every animal has to live. You know what? We're not Hindus, Mother.

MARGARET   Can't you see that they're just cats? God knows there's not much to them, but they live and breathe. Why do you hate them so much?

HAROLD   I don't hate cats. They could be zebras. Ostriches. I don't care. A yard full of anything is a problem. A yard full of bamboo-eating pandas!

MARGARET   You wouldn't shoot a panda.

HAROLD   Oh, no? If there's one creature with no apparent function on this planet, it's pandas. Except as a cuddly, stuffed animal for kids and a butt-scratching zoo specimen, what possible excuse can you offer for their existence? They're cute. That's it. That is it.

MARGARET   You're just plain ignorant. You know nothing about bio-diversity.

HAROLD   Oh, please! More Discovery Channel. Have you ever eaten panda? Has anyone every eaten panda? Do we need pandas to keep bamboo from overrunning the earth? They'll die off because they don't know how to look after themselves. Does a panda know one thing about survival? Do we even know what it is? Is it a bear? A raccoon? My advice, mother. Don't defend pandas. They eat only one thing, and what do they do all day when they're not eating bamboo? Make babies? I don't think so. Look at the panda population. They're lousy in bed. The zoos are working around the clock promoting panda sex. The pandas? They don't care.

MARGARET   We're talking about cats. And mother cats. And kittens. There are babies out there. Nursing babies.

HAROLD   Babies grow up to be cats. Look outside! Cats everywhere. And you, my dear, are a major contributor to the population explosion of adult cats. When do you start feeding the fleas? Wait. You already are. Feed one cat, feed a hundred fleas.

MARGARET   I don't want you to do this, Harold. It's immoral. I'm reluctant to use the word, but I think it's sinful.

HAROLD   So who are you? Mother Teresa of Vandalia? The patron saint of cats? This is not how you deal with cats. Jesus says something like the poor are always with you. This would be true for cats. If I thin out their ranks a little, the planet isn't going to tilt off its axis. The cats are always with us, but they don't all have to live in our yard on the dole. (*He leaves to another part of the house.*)

MARGARET   (*Going to the table to sit, taking her notebook from a pocket, and speaking aloud as she writes.*) A cat can be anywhere. The safest place in the world for a cat is in a place where it can't be seen, a dark place, like under a bed, where all it has to do is close its eyes and it's gone. (*During this time,* HAROLD *reappears in the doorway, listens, and then leaves.*) The safest place in the world for a cat is in a place full of beautiful smells, like a field of flowers, where all it has to do is fold its flower petal ears around its nose, and around its stamen whiskers, and sway in the breeze like a cat in bloom. The safest place in the world for a cat is in a very high place where it can't be reached, like a tall fir tree, where all it has to do is stretch out on the topmost branch in the sun, but maybe with one eye on the eagles. Or snoozing in the cradle of the new moon, where all it has to do is circle the blue earth, and even the eagles can't fly so high. A cat can be anywhere. They're sometimes hard to find.

HAROLD comes into the kitchen again, getting himself a glass of water from the refrigerator. When she hears him, she puts her notebook away again.

HAROLD   Are you still leaving in the morning with Sally? (*She appears not to hear him.*) Mother. Mother. I asked you a question.

MARGARET   Yes?

HAROLD   Is Sally still picking you up in the morning?

MARGARET   Yes.

HAROLD   Are you really going to Sally's?

MARGARET   You're asking if I'm lying to you.

HAROLD   No, I'm just making sure I know what's happening.

MARGARET   Where else would I go?

HAROLD   That's a question I'm not allowed to ask.

MARGARET   Yes, and have I ever lied to you about where I go?

HAROLD   Technically, no, you haven't.

MARGARET   Technically?

HAROLD   You never tell me where you disappear to, and then you're back, as if nothing has happened, as if you haven't been gone.

MARGARET   Well?

HAROLD   As if everything is just fine, all normal, when it's not normal at all.

MARGARET   What isn't?

HAROLD   The way you disappear. The way you just vanish—sometimes for weeks, once for a whole month. And I'm to act as though it's just a part of life, like a vacation, or a common cold, that just happens, and then it's over.

MARGARET   And over it is. That's all it is. And that's all there is to say.

HAROLD   Tell Sally to come early. She doesn't need to come in.

MARGARET   She won't come in.

HAROLD   And keep this cat problem just between us. You don't need to involve her in this.

MARGARET   I don't need to.

HAROLD   Good.

MARGARET   But I will.

HAROLD   Please, Mother.

MARGARET   What you need to do is to get her opinion. Invite her to lunch at the cafe and tell her about the cats. Don't argue the case in court. Just describe the situation and let her react. You know you used to talk to her about everything. She was your confidant. You used to listen to her more than you did to me.

HAROLD   I don't see how we can ever get back there.

MARGARET   It's not about getting back there. It's about getting past this. You should try.

HAROLD   I don't know where to begin. That man she was married to—

MARGARET   It might help if you didn't always refer to him as "that man." Give him his name back. Let him be a person. He hurt her, but she needs to be able to talk about David with some humanity.

HAROLD   That man was the scum of the earth. What he did was unforgivable. And she couldn't see what he was. She defended him even when he stole from the bank. Always the rescuer. And you know what? She turned her back on her family and—

MARGARET   He was her family. He was her husband. But five years, Harold, five years. Maybe what we all do is unforgivable, but somehow we have to forgive just the same. We have to forgive each other.

HAROLD   Do you forgive me?

MARGARET   Constantly.

HAROLD   Constantly?

MARGARET   It's a full-time job, Harold.

HAROLD   Am I such a difficult person? (*MARGARET doesn't reply.*) What does Sally think of me?

MARGARET   Talk to her yourself. Do you know that she loves you?

HAROLD   How can she?

MARGARET   Sometimes you're not very lovable, but I know she does love you. And sometimes she wants to take you by the ears and twist them till you fall to your knees and beg for mercy.

HAROLD   Has she said that?

MARGARET   No, but I know I'd like to take you by the ears—

HAROLD   Please, Mother—

MARGARET   And I think she'd like you to be more humble and—

HAROLD   I'm beyond humility.

MARGARET   Yes.

HAROLD   I need you to help me with Sally.

MARGARET   How much are you willing to do?

HAROLD   I don't know. (*He is silent for a time.*) I guess I asked you about mail.

MARGARET   Yes, you did.

HAROLD   I take it there's nothing for me.

MARGARET   As a matter of fact, there is. (*She takes an envelope from her one of her pockets.*) I thought this was just some charity solicitation. It appears to be some family search company. Parents. Children. It's called Family Reunion. I didn't read it. It's stained. I had thrown it out, but then I got to thinking about you being so anxious. (*She hands him an envelope and goes to work at the sink, as if to give him space.*)

HAROLD   I have not been anxious, Mother. (*HAROLD opens the letter and reads it.*) God in heaven! (*He reads again, putting it down, then picking it up. He looks stricken.*)

MARGARET   (*Without turning to look.*) Well, is it what you've been waiting for? (*When he doesn't reply, she turns and sees the look on his face. She quickly comes over to him.*) What in the world is wrong? Talk to me. (*Without speaking, HAROLD folds the letter, gets up slowly, as though defeated, and leaves the room. She stands for a while, staring after him, and then returns to the table to resume writing in her notebook.*)

In the beginning there was an only cat as large as a planet. As huge as a star. No, it was larger than that. It was as large as a galaxy. No, it was larger than that. If you took all the galaxies in the universe and strung them together, they would be almost as long as its tail. No one knows just how the only cat became two cats. Or when the two cats became other cats. Or when the other cats became kittens. Or when the only cat became white cats and then gray cats and then black cats, or when it surprised itself one morning and woke up yellow cats, or when the cats climbed up a tree and became spotted cats and then jumped down, became striped cats, and disappeared into the grass. A very, very old and only cat with teeth millions of years old tries to tell you this story, but it sometimes falls asleep before it can tell its very, very long tale.

END OF SCENE

Act I, Scene 3: Early dawn the next morning.
Outside a loud clanging noise erupts, the ringing of a large dinner bell and a banging on a large pot, as margaret *sounds an alarm in the yard to drive the cats away before* HAROLD *can shoot them.* HAROLD *comes into the kitchen, crosses to the porch door, opens it, and listens.*

HAROLD   Mother! Mother! There are people still sleeping on this street. Come inside.
When MARGARET *comes into the kitchen, she is dressed somewhat formally, as if for a public event. She puts on an apron and begins to fix breakfast at the counter, ignoring* HAROLD.
HAROLD   Well, are they gone? Have all the cats been driven out of Iowa? You know you have them trained. They'll expect food. (*She continues to ignore him.*) How soon are we going to have breakfast?
MARGARET   (*Without turning to look at him.*) You'll have it when you have it. (HAROLD *stands looking at her. She is silent for a moment.*) You have dinners for the next few days in the refrigerator and the freezer, and milk for breakfast, and there's cereal in the pantry. You'll probably eat lunch at the cafe, but there's food enough here if you want it. And your prescriptions are all refilled.
HAROLD   You're rehearsing for your death.
MARGARET   What are you talking about?
HAROLD   All these years. You're practicing.
MARGARET   How psychiatric!
HAROLD   Well? (*She ignores him.*) Call me when it's ready. (*He goes*

into another part of the house. When MARGARET *sees that he's gone,
she goes to the porch door to look into the yard.* HAROLD *returns to the
kitchen, carrying an army fatigue jacket, a double-barreled shotgun,
and a box of shells.* MARGARET *recoils when she sees him. He lays the
shotgun and shells on the table and steps out onto the porch.* MARGARET
*approaches the table and puts her hand on the stock of the shotgun. She
picks the shotgun up awkwardly.* HAROLD *comes back into the kitchen,
wearing the jacket. They stand very still, looking at each other in
silence.*)

HAROLD   Careful! Be careful with that weapon. (*He takes the shot-
gun from her, picks up the box of shells, and lays them on the floor by
the door.*) It's not loaded, but you never know. (MARGARET *returns to
the counter where she resumes preparing breakfast, but after a mo-
ment she stops what she's doing, takes off her apron, hangs it in the
pantry, and leaves the room.* HAROLD *goes to the refrigerator, opens the
door, and is looking for food when* MARGARET *reappears, carrying two
suitcases. He watches her cross to the porch doorway, where she sets the
suitcases down.*)

MARGARET   (*About to speak when the phone rings.*) Yes, I'm ready....
What happened? Oh, my! (*She hangs up.*)

HAROLD   Is she coming?

MARGARET   Yes, she's coming.

HAROLD   She's coming, so she called to tell you she's coming?

MARGARET   She'll be a little late.

HAROLD   What a surprise!

MARGARET   She never does anything right. Always your little digs.

HAROLD   She's ever been on time for anything. Am I right?

MARGARET   And you've never been late for anything.

HAROLD   Never. Am I right?

MARGARET   And that's such an admirable goal.

HAROLD   I'd rather be half-an-hour early than—

MARGARET   Please, don't ever say that again.

HAROLD   Well, it's true.

MARGARET   You've made up your mind to do this.

HAROLD   And you know what? I should have done it sooner.

MARGARET   You're not going to talk it through with Sally.

HAROLD   I don't see the point.

MARGARET   And you say you sincerely want a reconciliation with her.

HAROLD   By dragging her into this? How does that work?

MARGARET   It gives you a reason to talk. You haven't found a way on your own.

HAROLD   It's a bad idea. Don't bag up these cats with what's going on between me and Sally.

MARGARET   You really do see this as something separate, something isolated from everything else going on around you.

HAROLD   It's about cats.

MARGARET   We have lived together for almost fifty years, and yet we don't seem to live in the same world. I don't know how that happened.

HAROLD   Nothing happened.

MARGARET   Maybe what happened is that nothing happened. Like two pillars on a porch.

HAROLD   Back to the cats.

MARGARET   I know that you take me for granted. I've made that easy for you. I have stood by you. I have been loyal. Sometimes, I think, blindly loyal. I have listened to you justify every step of your life. You probably didn't even think I was listening.

HAROLD   I have always valued your opinion.

MARGARET   You have always wanted my proxy.

HAROLD   That's not true.

MARGARET   I have asked for very little, and I have insisted on even less. I have waited on you when at times I would rather have not, and I have agreed with you when I didn't agree with you. But I have lived an otherwise aimless life in my little corner, merely wishing for more with all my books and magazines about Karthoum and Kinshasa and Bombay and Bangkok and La Paz and Santiago and Tierra del Fuego and—

HAROLD   Your disappearances—

MARGARET   Not one place I'll ever see. And my useless way of tracking the news of the world. I seem to care so much about the news, but the news takes no notice of whether I'm paying attention. Nowhere lives there a more totally passive creature. I don't make news. I don't even witness it. I live life third hand. I just read about it and hear about it from other witnesses.

HAROLD   It's always interested you.

MARGARET   Now there's an epitaph. "She was interested." And then I ask myself what else a woman does in a little, dozing town like this when her husband provides and provides and provides. I am so ashamed of my life.

HAROLD   Now, Mother, you don't have to apologize for—

MARGARET   But you need to know that I have my limits. Even I, the world's most absorbent cleaning cloth, mop, sponge—

HAROLD   We all have our limits, Mother, we all—

MARGARET   But you have never seen the end of me.

HAROLD   We all have our limits. We live in a world of limits. We're surrounded by county lines, township lines, property lines, and driveway and porch lines. We live on a street of peaceful people. We live limited lives of moderation and civility, where all we ever smell is rain and sweet mown grass, and the good burnt smell of bottle rockets on the Fourth of July, but not cat urine. (*Pleading with her.*) Not cat urine, Mother! The cats are pissing on everything!

MARGARET   I hate that word!

HAROLD   I hate that smell. And it is what it is. Cat piss!

MARGARET   You should know that I intend to found a refuge for cats. Not something grand. A quiet little sanctuary for cats and kittens.

HAROLD   This is that Italian operation, isn't it?

MARGARET   No, it's Iowa. But do you know the domestic cat lived in Italy back before the Romans as early as the ninth century, BC?

HAROLD   So what?

MARGARET   There's a kinship with a long history. I'd set up a kind of foster home with donors and volunteers. And it would work as an adoption agency.

HAROLD   Mother Dobson's Book of Pipe Dreams. Stainless steel kitchens that cost more than a house used to cost, travels around the world to places people in Vandalia never heard of and can't spell, and now social work with cats. Cats. Why cats? (*Standing in the doorway to the porch.*) What species is more thankless? (*Yelling into the yard.*) Can somebody tell me what a cat does? Let's give this thing some perspective, Mother. A few cats, more or less. What difference does it make, for God's sake? We're fighting a global war against terrorism.

MARGARET   You said this was about cats. Nothing else.

HAROLD   It is. I never said otherwise. It's about these pointless hairballs that lie around and blink at you and give you these cunning cat smiles and rub against your pant leg and make you think you've got a new best friend.

MARGARET   I'm going to call it Catmandu, with a C, which will sound silly to you, but what idea of mine doesn't? I know you think I've been a hobby addict. And I can see how you'd think it's just one more. But this idea is more than a hobby, and, anyway, a hobby isn't a crime, is it? Not even your awful collection of Jim Beam bourbon bottles shaped like race cars and oil derricks and elephants.

HAROLD   Bourbon doesn't smell like cat piss. Now, then, we're going to set aside this grand plan, Mother. It's nothing that you'll ever see through. I have allowed the stench of cats to soak into the ground until it's rising through the roots of the trees and the shrubs and even the grass. It's systemic. Be glad we're not on well water. Understand that I blame myself for letting it go this far, but no longer will I neglect this house and this yard.

MARGARET   I've heard too many patriotic speeches from you over too many years on individual rights, respect for individual rights, equality, but I take it that I don't qualify.

HAROLD   (*Picking up the shotgun and the box of shells and standing in the doorway to the porch.*) Cats don't qualify. Cats don't have it in their nature to act like Americans. And they're not teachable. They enter our yard and they live among us until they take over our lives. We come home one day and find that the life we live has been overrun. Stop looking at me like I'm crazy. (*Turns toward the porch.*) They are exalted for a little while, but are gone and brought low; they are cut off as the tops of the ears of corn.

MARGARET   I had no idea you were filled with such hatred. And lunacy. Hateful lunacy!

HAROLD   We do what we have to do! Necessity! Necessity! Stay the course! (*He strides out on the porch. and a few moments later there are several shotgun blasts. Then silence.* MARGARET *sits at the table, her hands over her ears. More shots are fired, and she flinches, then runs from the kitchen into the hallway. After a few moments,* HAROLD *reappears, laying the shotgun and box of shells on the table.*)

HAROLD   There. That's a start. (*He looks around and sees that she has gone. He goes to the doorway to the hall. He returns to the table, empties spent shells from the shotgun, and begins to clean it.* MARGARET *reenters the kitchen.*) Maybe now we can begin to get on with our lives.

MARGARET   (*Crossing to the porch door as if in a trance.*) You murder them. You murder me. I am dead to you. (*She picks up her suitcases and leaves onto the porch.*)

HAROLD   (*Getting up, going to the porch doorway, and calling.*) We do what we have to do! We stay the course!

CURTAIN

Act II: Near the end of May.
Scene 1: Late morning.

HAROLD *talks on a cordless phone, pacing around the kitchen and nervously shuffling magazines, newspapers, dishes, and fast food bags on the cluttered counter and table. He wears a T-shirt, baggy pants, and slippers. As he paces, he has to avoid falling over a camp cot in the middle of the kitchen, piled with blankets and a few pillows.*

HAROLD   I have no idea. . . . You wouldn't think so, would you, Clarence? Yeah, yeah, yeah, it's becoming a way of life in the business world. . . . No. . . . I wouldn't approve that loan if he were my own brother. But it's none of my business, is it? . . . What can I say? . . . Just bring it to a conclusion. There's too much unfinished business in America today, too much unfinished business in the world. You know what I mean? . . . We get up enough nerve to start something, and then we start second-guessing ourselves. Well, maybe we should have done this. No, no, wait a minute, think it over, maybe we should have done that. Let's not press ahead with the plan because we might make a serious mistake. And you know what? It's called the Korean War Syndrome. . . . Okay, Clarence. Stand your ground. . . . Sure, sure, just don't call me late to dinner. Oh, by the way, some guy from Omaha called and wants to talk to me about investing in a fast food franchise. . . . He said you mentioned my name. . . . Look, I'm not looking for a late-life career in French fries. . . . Well, whatever. . . . Potato Babies? . . . Geez, Clarence, Potato Babies! It's all grease. It's all grease to me. Got that, Clarence? (*He puts the phone down on the table and stares out the window. He returns to the table and begins looking for something. He moves a pile of newspapers on top of the phone and sorts unsuccessfully through a stack of bills, reciting from memory.*) "—in the drawers of the dresser of walnut and brass, in the cartons, scarred suitcases, piled in the corner." (*After throwing the bills down in frustration, he goes to the refrigerator and forages, and again recites from memory.*) "As she crawled on her knees through the dust of the attic, she paused by a fat box, a very round, red box, a very large red box of hats that was busy, though most people think that a box is a box, and a box doesn't think, and a box can't be busy—" (*The phone rings, and it takes him some time to track it down.*) YEH-low! . . . Yes, it is . . . fine, just fine, and you? . . . Well, you know what, Mrs. Dabney, she is not here. . . . I'm afraid I don't know the answer to that. . . . You're supposed to know everything in this town, but you don't know where my wife is. . . . Just a statement of fact, Mrs. Dabney, just a statement of fact. . . . Well, sure, I can do that, but in the meantime, you should stop acting like you don't know what's going on. (*He puts the phone down.*) The phoney old prospector, panning for gossip. (*He sits down at the table. On a newspaper open on the floor beside his chair stands a pair of old army boots and some shoe-polishing materials. He begins polishing a boot, humming and singing occasional phrases.*) "Baum, baum, baum, baum, and the chapel bells were ringing . . . in the little valley town, and the song . . . that they were singing, was for little Jimmy Brown." (*Shifts to the song "Volare."*) ". . . oh, oh, cantare, oh, oh, oh, oh. Nel blu, dipinto, di blu." What the hell does that mean? "Dipinto, di blu?" (*He throws down the boot and the cloth and sits with his head in his hands. In a voice of near anguish, he recites rough paraphrases of verses on Job's suffering.*) The sparks fly upward, and I will die like a groveling cat, its tongue in the dust. (*He stands and throws up his arms in despair.*) "For the thing which I greatly feared is come upon me, and I am full of tossings to and fro until the dawning of the day. I should have been as though I had not been, straight from the womb to the grave." (*He lies down on the cot as though exhausted, but then the phone rings, and, after ignoring it, he finally rises and picks up the phone.*) "—and I am full of tossings to and fro until the dawning of the day." No, I was just sort of talking to myself, Sally. . . . Your mother's not here. She's supposed to be with you. . . . Today? . . . Now? I appreciate you letting me know. . . . No, I'm not going to start an argument with her. . . . You have my word, but if she starts an argument with me, am I supposed to— . . . So I'm supposed to turn belly up. . . . Sally? YEH-low? (*He puts the phone down, stares at the floor, then around the kitchen, and then gets up and begins anxiously trying to recover some order in the kitchen. His efforts are disorganized and not very productive. He wraps up the boots and polish and throws them into the pantry. Then he notices the camp cot and bedding and clumsily carries them out of the kitchen and returns.*) Like a groveling cat, its tongue in the dust. (*He tries quickly to empty the sink, putting some of the dishes into a trash bag. As he does this,* MARGARET *opens the porch door. His back is to her, and he does not hear her come in.*)

MARGARET   I didn't expect you to be here. You're usually at the bank. (*She starts to leave.*)

HAROLD   No, no, you don't have to leave.

MARGARET   I just came for a few things. Some clothes, mostly.

HAROLD   Come in. Come in. I'm in the middle of cleaning house. Cleaning day.

MARGARET   (*Looking around the kitchen.*) You'll need more than a day.

HAROLD   No hurry. It only gets dirty again. What brings you to town?

MARGARET   Clothes. And I need to pick up some of my cookbooks. And a few cooking utensils. If I can find them. You don't mind?

HAROLD   No, no, not at all. Did Sally drive you?

MARGARET   I've renewed my license. Sally let me use her car.

HAROLD   Driving again! Well, how about that! Hit anybody? Any tickets yet?

MARGARET   I'm not here to review my driving record.

HAROLD   No, no, I understand that. None of my business. (*MARGA-RET goes into the pantry and nearly falls over the army boots.*) Sorry, I'm sorry. Just a little project I'm in the middle of. (*He kneels in the doorway of the pantry to try to recover his boots, as she turns to come out. She waits, while he moves aside.*) Cup of coffee? I can fix some lunch.

MARGARET   (*Walking to the desk, carrying a shopping bag, into which she begins putting some cookbooks.*) Thank you, no. I didn't expect you to be here. I didn't really want you to be here.

HAROLD   I live here, Mother.

MARGARET   Don't call me that.

HAROLD   It's who you are.

MARGARET   Don't call me that.

HAROLD   What would you prefer me to call you?

MARGARET   Nothing.

HAROLD   Be reasonable, M—okay, okay. Just be reasonable.

MARGARET   How would you know even the first thing about being reasonable?

HAROLD   Maybe I over-reacted. I mean to the cat problem.

MARGARET   There was a folder of recipes here. A yellow folder.

HAROLD   I have not touched any of your cooking stuff.

MARGARET   Well, it was here. On this shelf, next to this book.

HAROLD   I do not know.

MARGARET   And I didn't see a single one of my cats out there.

HAROLD   The rest of them left. Gone. They're off the dole.

MARGARET   (*Looking for cooking utensils in a large drawer.*) Where are the other cats?

HAROLD   You left. Did you expect them to hang around and starve? Without a government subsidy, they all got jobs.

MARGARET   There is nothing, nothing about what happened that warrants your sarcasm.

HAROLD   Well, they're gone, as far as I can tell.

MARGARET   Is anything clean in this kitchen? (*She clears the sink and then throws dirty utensils into the sink to wash them.*)

HAROLD   I told you I'm in the process of cleaning.

MARGARET   I'm taking these things with me. Clean.

HAROLD   Are you going to start emptying out the house?

MARGARET   People say that you live in a pigpen.

HAROLD   I'm the one who lives in this house. And you know what? It's nobody else's business.

MARGARET   Squalor. But you're right. It's your torpor.

HAROLD   Doesn't Sally have a kitchen? With drawers? Every kitchen has this stuff.

MARGARET   I'm cooking for her. And I'm teaching her to cook.

HAROLD   She hates to cook.

MARGARET   She wants to learn. (*She walks to the desk.*) And I also need my kitchen design books. They were all here.

HAROLD   They're gone.

MARGARET   What did you do with them?

HAROLD   You left. Maybe I threw them out. I don't know.

MARGARET   This is my kitchen.

HAROLD   (*Angrily, his voice rising.*) Not anymore. You left this kitchen. And you left me.

MARGARET   This will always be my kitchen.

HAROLD   Then why don't you use it?

MARGARET   Because you are in it. You are in this house.

HAROLD   It's my house.

MARGARET   Fine. Live here like a wild animal. It suits you. (*She drags the kitchen trashcan into the center of the kitchen and begins rapidly sorting and throwing things away.*) In the meantime, I'm going to have Sally's kitchen redone. Your daughter is going to have the kitchen that I always wanted.

HAROLD   And how do you propose to pay for that?

MARGARET   You're going to pay for it.

HAROLD   I won't.

MARGARET   You wouldn't do this for me, but you will do it for Sally. And why should you even care? Our bank accounts are full. We can't get any more money into our bank accounts.

HAROLD   They're not piggy banks, Mother. Nor are they bottomless.

MARGARET   (*Wagging a finger at him.*) Uh-uh-uh. We have assets which you don't even remember. Property which I have never seen.

HAROLD   We didn't get to this point by pouring thirty-thousand dollars into a magazine kitchen.

MARGARET   But we are at this point. Or do you intend to sit around in this filthy kitchen, piling up frozen dinner trays and counting your assets till the day you die? (*She throws a stack of meal trays, napkins, and plastic cups into the trash.*)

HAROLD   We used to say it was a virtue to save. We used to call it thrift. And you know what? We used to think it was actually a good thing.

MARGARET   But you've become miserly.

HAROLD   People max out their credit cards, and when they do, they get more credit cards. Oh, Lord, I don't belong in this world of massive debt and designer kitchens. (*While he is pacing and gesturing, MARGARET finds a letter in the pile on the table, turns her back to HAROLD to glance at the contents, looks up at HAROLD to see if he is watching, and puts the letter in her purse.*) I was born seventy years too late. People want a microwave the size of an airplane hanger and a stainless-steel walk-in refrigerator and a six-burner range that sucks all the oxygen out of the air. No one needs to live like that. No one should want to live like that.

MARGARET I'm going to redo Sally's kitchen.

HAROLD (*Striding around in disgust.*) Fine, fine and dandy! Do it! Run up a debt. See what happens!

MARGARET Are you going to shoot Sally's kitchen?

HAROLD You said sarcasm was off limits.

MARGARET I'd strongly advise you not to interfere with what I'm going to do for Sally.

HAROLD What is that supposed to mean?

MARGARET It would not be in your best interest.

HAROLD And what is that supposed to mean?

MARGARET I don't want to have this discussion. Not here. And not now.

HAROLD You're dropping hints, some kind of a threat, and I want to know what you're up to.

MARGARET There's no point in my talking directly to you, because you don't listen to me.

HAROLD All right, all right, I'll listen to you.

MARGARET Why would you? The sound of my voice is nothing but syllables, just a lot of background static in that brain of yours. And I don't know when it was ever anything more. You don't hear me.

HAROLD I hear you.

MARGARET You hear you.

HAROLD Sally was right. I give up.

MARGARET Sally?

HAROLD Never mind.

MARGARET When did you talk to her?

HAROLD She called. She said there's no point in arguing with you.

MARGARET She said that?

HAROLD And she was right. Your mind's made up. What's the point?

MARGARET She told you not to provoke an argument. She knows you.

HAROLD   When are you coming home to stay?

MARGARET   I don't know.

HAROLD   You should come home.

MARGARET   Should?

HAROLD   This is your home. I'm your husband.

MARGARET   What a comfort those words are.

HAROLD   Those are true words, and you should abide by them. That's what's failed us in this country. We've lost the will, we've lost the courage to abide.

MARGARET   Please don't sing the hymn.

HAROLD   An abiding home, an abiding family. Abidance. Can you think of any better way to say what's gone from this great land of ours? Abidance! And it's been happening for half a century. We were half-asleep when the NKPA crossed into South Korea. My 24th Division was there in no time, and all we did was get run over for six weeks—ill-equipped, under-trained, defective rifles, guys wiping cosmoline off their weapons, which did a lot of good when all you had was a dozen rounds. Taejon! What a slaughterhouse! They caught General Dean, but they didn't catch me. We were scrambling around in the mountains with no idea what hit us. Within a week half of us were dead or wounded. Eight thousand men! But we fought back, and we made a war of it. Inchon was a textbook lesson in putting men ashore under the most godawful conditions! But for what! A year later, we were beating their asses, but we stopped and sat on chairs at the negotiating table while our men went on fighting senseless battles, dying in the mountains in the bitter cold. We second-guessed ourselves and turned our backs on the Korean people. And we turned our backs on the people of South Vietnam. And we couldn't finish the Gulf War. Does anyone in America really think we have the stomach to stay the course in Iraq and see this war on terrorism to the finish? The country's weak. From Washington on down. You see it right here in our own local government. Irresolute leaders with irresolute judgment. The county's turning brown. We can't even deal with the immigrant problem. We are unable to abide. Men turn their backs on economic and social problems, on each other, on their marriages, their wives, and their children. Does anyone remember the Greatest Generation? That generation did truly abide. It did what had to be done, and somehow we have got to get back there. Back to the way it was. Back to life as it was. Now, then—

MARGARET   Life as it was, life as it was. Wouldn't it be nice if—

HAROLD   Two words. Douglas MacArthur. That man knew what it meant to abide. When my squad was camped on the . . . the . . . I thought I'd never forget the name of that river. It was the spring of 1952, and for weeks we were filthy with mud and sweat and the parasites of Southeast Asia. We were ordered to stay out of that river because it was a torrent of winter runoff, but we were just boys, and we wanted to get clean, we wanted to jump into the old swimmin' hole, and the next thing Bill Jansen and Ernie Grabowski and I knew, we were a mile downstream, fighting for our lives, exhausted, gulping water, trying to stay afloat, and do you know what? I was wondering what my mother would say when she heard I'd gone for a swim and drowned in some Korean river, drowned like a schoolboy in a damned swimming accident, but on the other side of the world, and I made up my mind I wasn't going to do that to my mother. If I was going to die, it was going to be on my terms. Death had to mean something.

MARGARET   So you found a way to abide.

HAROLD   I'm standing here. I'm telling the story. I did abide.

MARGARET   You did, indeed. And this story and all its trappings are somehow supposed to be the gold standard by which I am to be judged and governed.

HAROLD   Governed?

MARGARET   You set yourself up as the grand measure by which people are to abide. By which I am to abide. Your rules. You have your rules, but your rules are also rules of slaughter. All your talk of near-drowning and abiding and family bonds doesn't seem to include me and the things that are dear to me. You think that you can dictate the terms of our last years. You think that after my little walkout, I'll just come home and be the good servant as though nothing ever happened. I haven't been everything I could have been. I've no doubt bored you. I've no doubt been less charming than some of the women in your life. Maybe I'll live another ten years. Maybe twenty. But like this? Never. Shuffling around the kitchen at the age of ninety, serving you over-easy eggs or cold slaw or creamed corn? I'd rather go to sleep and never wake up. I'd rather walk out the door and get lost in the cemetery. I'd rather—

HAROLD   As you often have walked out the door and gotten lost. I wish you'd say what you mean. I wish you'd—

MARGARET   You don't listen. Look at us, Harold. We're old. Nothing is so pathetic as two old people repeating themselves, repeating bad habits, repeating their petty, abusive ways, mauling each other with maudlin memories. There's nothing so cruel as our petty, daily tyrannies. But then to slaughter my poor, innocent cats and kittens! When I see what you've become, I think what couldn't you do?

HAROLD   This is way out of proportion to any—

MARGARET   Be still and listen! I think—I have thought to myself that I have been your accomplice. I helped you do this thing.

HAROLD   Shoot cats?

MARGARET   Yes, yes, and everything that's gone before it, everything that's led up to it.

HAROLD   You know what? I think you've been around cats too long. Something in the way you talk just circles around things with its tail switching. A cat meows out of the corner of its mouth. It pretends to be content. All those cats in the yard. They prowled around in sleeper cells. Cunning, terror, terrorism—

MARGARET   You don't listen. You don't even listen to yourself, because if you did, you would hear how—

HAROLD   All right, all right, Margaret, let's try to—

MARGARET   Why am I even standing here as if something intelligible might come out of all this? I came here to get my rolling pin. My rolling pin! (*She begins to gather up the things she has come for and moves toward the door.*) And I'm arguing with a deranged old man who is lecturing me on the Korean War and terrorist cats. You think the planet is falling apart. You think it's going to hell. But it's you, Harold. It's happening to you. (*She opens the porch door and sets her bags outside.*) It's happened to you. (*She leaves.*)

HAROLD   Imjin. (*Calling to Margaret.*) The Imjin River. It was the Imjin.

END OF SCENE

Act II, Scene 2: Evening, a few weeks later in early June.
The kitchen is now cleaner and more organized than in early June. HAROLD *has set the table for an evening meal, with napkins, candles, and a center-piece of flowers. As a romantic, orchestral recording plays softly,* HAROLD *nervously transfers food from some bowls and plates to other bowls and plates. He puts a few dishes into the oven, then carries empty bowls, wicker baskets, and dish towels into the pantry and closes the pantry door. When he hears a knock at the door to the porch, he looks around the kitchen, hastily puts on an apron, and goes to the door.*

HAROLD   (*With expansive charm.*) Welcome to your house. Come in!

MARGARET   Am I early?

HAROLD   No, you're right on time.

MARGARET   Something smells very good.

HAROLD   We're nearly ready to eat. (*He curtseys to call attention to his apron.*) How do I look?

MARGARET   To be honest, it makes you look fat. No, really, it looks fine, though I wouldn't wear it with that shirt. You look like a cheerleader. School colors. But it's a nice thought. Are you trying to make me feel at home?

HAROLD   I'm glad you decided to come for dinner. I've been hoping and praying that we could work this out.

MARGARET   You in prayer. And you in an apron.

HAROLD   (*Pulling out a chair at the table.*) Please, sit down! I'm just going to bring everything to the table, and then we can sit together and talk. (*He begins bringing dishes of food to the table.*)

MARGARET   The tiger lilies are very nice. Where did you find them?

HAROLD   Out along the river road. They're everywhere.

MARGARET   (*Looking at them a long time, and touching the blossoms.*) The color of country drives on Sundays, lily leaves drooping over, long shadows of the afternoon falling across the roads of my childhood.

HAROLD   Long shadows. That's a pretty gloomy memory.

MARGARET   I loved those drives. We'd stop at a country crossroads with no other car in sight, and we'd all get out, and I'd reach out my arms to all the green fields growing and the cloud-feathered sky and the silent-running river, and I would draw the summer into my lungs, and it would fill my blood until some of it spilled from my eyes.

HAROLD   That's quite a memory,

MARGARET   I can't say that I ever cried about anything like that.

MARGARET   Well, it was a kind of crying.

HAROLD   (*Sitting down.*) How many kinds are there? People cry. (*He tucks in his napkin.*)

MARGARET   People sniffle. Sometimes tears fall in silence. People sob. They wail, shriek, cry until they laugh, laugh until they cry.

HAROLD   (*Tucking his napkin into his collar.*) Now, then. Let me serve you a little of everything.

MARGARET   You don't have to play the waiter.

HAROLD   Okay, then help yourself to things. What have I forgotten?

MARGARET   I'll get us some water.

HAROLD   No, no, no. Stay where you are. You're the guest of honor. (*He goes to the refrigerator.*) You know what? I had our water poured, and then I forgot to bring it to the table.

MARGARET   I haven't heard this music in years.

HAROLD   Hank Mancini.

MARGARET   Hank? Are you trying to woo me with this nostalgia concert?

HAROLD   I'm not trying to woo you.

MARGARET   Flowers? And an entire meal?

HAROLD   Well, it's nothing to take a picture of.

MARGARET   It's very nice. Thank you. I'm amazed that you've pre-pared all these dishes. You learned to cook.

HAROLD   I wouldn't really say that. I can read a cookbook.

MARGARET   Green bean casserole. Potato salad. Fried chicken. Biscuits. Green peas, Spanish peanuts, and sour cream. All the comforts of a church potluck.

HAROLD   I didn't think this would be the time for experiment. Start with the basics, right?

MARGARET   Canned green beans. U-m-m-m! Just the way Robbie Harrison does it.

HAROLD   She opens a can?

MARGARET   Robbie takes shortcuts. Did you get her recipe?

HAROLD   You could say that.

MARGARET   (*Smelling the potato salad on her fork.*) Here's a familiar smell. (*Tasting.*) Horseradish. Well, this really is a comfort. Ger-aldine Harper always uses horseradish. Harold, you've been busy. Did everyone in town know you were preparing dinner?

HAROLD   I wouldn't be surprised.

MARGARET   Let's see who else's recipe I can identify. This green pea salad. U-m-m-m-m! Lots of ginger. Lots of Florence York. Did you use the entire church's cookbook?

HAROLD   Well, not exactly.

MARGARET   (*Setting down her fork and rising.*) Is there anything on this table that you actually prepared yourself? Did you cook anything?

HAROLD   I don't know how to cook.

MARGARET   But you wanted me to think you did. Didn't you?

HAROLD   I never said I cooked this meal.

MARGARET   (*Holding up the apron.*) You acted as though you did.

HAROLD   I set the table. I drove all over town to pick up this meal.

MARGARET   Meals on wheels!

HAROLD   I wasn't going to serve you an inedible meal.

MARGARET   I might have been sympathetic.

HAROLD   Don't pity me.

MARGARET   It would have been a start. It would have been a rare positive feeling, something to build on.

HAROLD   Good food is something to build on.

MARGARET   Other people's food. Did you pay them for it?

HAROLD   No. No one would accept anything.

MARGARET   Did you offer? Did you insist?

HAROLD   There are more important things for us to talk about.

MARGARET   More important than canned green bean casserole? I should say so. Like how the entire town of Vandalia is now catering our marriage problems. We're in full view. (*Opening the porch door.*)

HAROLD   They know what we're eating tonight.

MARGARET   And that we're eating together.

HAROLD   Why do you care? What difference does it make?

MARGARET   You're right. It doesn't. Everything is, as you would say, fine and dandy. Let's have an open house.

HAROLD   You're not angry with me anymore?

MARGARET   (*Closing the porch door loudly.*) Nothing's changed.

HAROLD   (*Rising.*) Then why did you come here tonight?

MARGARET   I believe it was you who invited me. I assume that you've got something more on your mind than fried chicken.

HAROLD   Shall we sit down? We have all this food, and you know what? There's a blueberry pie. Please, let's try to have this time together in a peaceful way. We can just talk. Let's just say we're having dinner.

MARGARET   (*Sitting down.*) Do you have ice cream for the blueberry pie?

HAROLD   We do. I didn't make it either. And neither did Phoebe Briggs.

MARGARET   You have dinner enough for a week.

HAROLD   (*Sitting down and tucking a napkin into his collar.*) Take some to Sally.

MARGARET   It's just plain odd.

HAROLD   What is?

MARGARET   (*Gesturing at the table and around the kitchen.*) This. All of this.

HAROLD   We're having dinner.

MARGARET   But like a courtship. Best behavior.

HAROLD   It wouldn't be so if you lived here.

MARGARET   If I lived here, one of us would be dead by now.

HAROLD   I'd like you to come home.

MARGARET   Coming home is far away, Harold, very far away. I can't see it from where I'm looking.

HAROLD   All those times over the years when you disappeared into your upper room, I never packed my bags and left.

MARGARET   You didn't need to. I was gone.

HAROLD   But don't you see how unnatural that was, Mother? (*She puts down her fork and stares into space.*) I'm sorry, I'm sorry. Margaret. Margaret. We've never really talked about this.

MARGARET   There was nothing to talk about. You knew where I was.

HAROLD   But the house was so empty. You were here, and you weren't here.

MARGARET   There was not one day, not one day, when I was living in my room that you did not have meals prepared for you and your shirts ironed and the floors vacuumed and—

HAROLD   (*Getting up from the table in frustration.*) But I never saw you for days. I'd come into the house, I'd hear your door closing, and then just silence. You were always slipping away—like a ghost. I'd hear little, distant, muffled sounds, a drawer pushed shut, water moving through the pipes, something falling on the bathroom tile—maybe a hairbrush. And then the dismal silence again.

MARGARET   After all these years, why bring it up now? We had an understanding that I would be left alone.

HAROLD   Understanding? I never understood it at all. I never had the slightest idea what—

MARGARET   I don't mean that. You agreed.

HAROLD   I went along with it.

MARGARET   You didn't have to "go along" with anything. You chose to. I didn't know why, but I wondered. Do you know?

HAROLD   I guess—I don't know—

MARGARET   You guess? Take a guess.

HAROLD   (*After a long silence.*) I guess I was afraid.

MARGARET   Afraid? Of what? Of me? Afraid of me! In all my years, I never would have guessed at that.

HAROLD   Not of you. For you. You would come down out of your room after days and nights without my seeing you, and you weren't—you seemed, well, not yourself, like somebody else. I didn't know who you were.

MARGARET   For heaven's sake! What are you talking about? First it's ghosts. Now it sounds like some kind of—like aliens in those tabloids.

HAROLD   Well, you know what? I don't know how to talk about it. I sometimes thought that you—I don't know, I don't know. (*He is silent for a long time, as if catatonic.*)

MARGARET   We'll talk about something else. Come and sit down.

HAROLD   (*Sits and pushes food around his plate.*) Does Sally have her new kitchen?

MARGARET   I'm sure you've been monitoring our bank accounts.

HAROLD   Does she use it?

MARGARET   I use it.

HAROLD   A six-burner range. Six burners.

MARGARET   And I'm sure you know the model number.

HAROLD   Is it everything that the magazines promise?

MARGARET   It's a kitchen.

HAROLD   No. This is a kitchen.

MARGARET   This is an artless room.

HAROLD   You used to like this room.

MARGARET   It's a dull room.

HAROLD   Well, it's still a kitchen. It's where you cook.

MARGARET   Where you cook?

HAROLD   It's where I live. The rest of the house is—it's just a dark—just—like a closet.

MARGARET   There are lights. And light switches. You can—

HAROLD   I don't go there anymore unless I have to.

MARGARET   Where do you sleep? (*HAROLD gestures around the kitchen.*) You sleep here? In the kitchen?

HAROLD   I have.

MARGARET   Where did you sleep last night? (*Again, HAROLD gestures around the kitchen.*) On what?

HAROLD   I have a cot.

MARGARET   A cot.

HAROLD   A camping cot.

MARGARET   Where is it? (*HAROLD points toward the inner doorway, and MARGARET goes to the doorway.*) I can't believe this. I thought things were getting better here, but you're living in a storm. In wreckage. You're being blown away.

HAROLD   You know what? I'm still here. Which is—

MARGARET   I'm not so sure you are here. Who's the ghost, Harold? Who's the ghost now?

HAROLD   You left me.

MARGARET   That doesn't explain anything.

HAROLD   How am I supposed to live here by myself?

MARGARET   You're not senile. You're not bed-ridden. Look at yourself. Just look at you, just—

HAROLD   This is killing me. It's killing me. I can't—

MARGARET   Everybody's dying, Harold. This is not an emergency—

HAROLD   It is an emergency. The lights are flashing all around us, the blue and—

MARGARET   I don't hear any sirens.

HAROLD   Because you're not here. You go away, like you always used to go away.

MARGARET   I never went away. I was always here, I was—

HAROLD   You were up in your damned room with those things you write, all those damned words, I never read so many words, pages and pages, notebooks full of—of stories and poems and all those—

MARGARET   You broke into my room.

HAROLD   (*Going to the desk, picking up a notebook, and holding it up for her to see.*) I didn't need to break into your room—

MARGARET   You broke into my room. You—

HAROLD   I opened the door. I had a key.

MARGARET   Since when?

HAROLD   I've always had a key.

MARGARET   I had a lock put on that door years ago.

HAROLD   I had a key.

MARGARET   And did you use it?

HAROLD   Not until now.

MARGARET   And did you find what you were looking for?

HAROLD   I don't know what I was looking for.

MARGARET   That is my room.

HAROLD   You don't live here anymore.

MARGARET   And have you destroyed my room—like the rest of this house?

HAROLD   No. I didn't touch it.

MARGARET   I don't believe that.

HAROLD   I didn't disturb anything. I just read things.

MARGARET   If you read it, you disturbed it.

HAROLD   Everything is just as it was.

MARGARET   What did you read?

HAROLD   I tried to read everything, but I couldn't stay in that room.

MARGARET   What do you mean?

HAROLD   It would get smaller.

MARGARET   What?

HAROLD   It got smaller.

MARGARET   (*Crossing to the porch door and opening it.*) My lord, Harold.

HAROLD   There are no hatboxes in the attic.

MARGARET   That's good to know.

HAROLD   Well, there aren't.

MARGARET   Imagine that. Not even one.

HAROLD   Not one. (*He opens the notebook.*)

MARGARET   (*Turning toward him.*) So?

HAROLD   Why would you write such things?

MARGARET   About what?

HAROLD   This stuff gives me the creeps.

MARGARET   (*Closing the porch door.*) This stuff. The creeps. That's your response, that's—

HAROLD   Here. Here's a perfect example. Some little girl—Sophie, you call her— crawls around in the attic. Things start to move and fly open. Hats fly around.

MARGARET   That's your version.

HAROLD   Now, then, listen. You have an entire shelf of this sort of thing. Maybe you can tell me what's going on. (*He reads from the notebook.*)

> When Sophie opened the door to the attic,
> though she didn't remember ever hearing
> even the thinnest whisker of sound,
> she did what she always did. She listened.

"Drawers of the dresser"—I'm going to skip through some of this—"drawers of the dresser of walnut and brass, . . . shined her small flashlight in circles, she saw something move and she heard something rustle, . . . and then there was silence, . . . chair by the window . . . an old summer evening, with moths on the screen of a grandmother's dreaming . . . . a fat box, a very round, red box—

> a very large red box of hats that was busy,
> though most people think that a box is a box,
> and a box doesn't think, and a box can't be busy,
> but this box of hats was her grandmother's hatbox. . . ."

(*Pausing and looking at* MARGARET.) There is no hatbox in the attic. Anyway, then "the lid rose straight upward, bounced off of the rafters, and Sophie fell backward, her eyes big as platters . . . until something started that's hard to imagine. . . ." Hard to imagine? Where does this silliness come from?

MARGARET   Nowhere. Anywhere. It just comes. I'm not a psychiatrist. And you may think it's silly. I don't care.

HAROLD   Is this all you wrote?

MARGARET   That's not how it ends. Obviously.

HAROLD   What's the point? What could possibly be the point?

MARGARET   It's pointess. It's silly. You don't really want to know.

HAROLD   I'm asking.

MARGARET   Truly. You don't want to know.

HAROLD   Look, I'm trying to understand you, I'm trying to take an interest in—

MARGARET   You don't need to understand me. You've lived with me for nearly fifty years, and now you go into my room to read about me. Now that—that—is what you might call silliness. I'm a breathing human being, for heaven's sake, not some words on a page.

HAROLD   There may be more of you in that closet of yours upstairs than there is in this kitchen.

> . . . this sleeping red hatbox
> had started to dream that it wasn't a hatbox,
> a dream so amazing the butterfly ribbon
> began to untie itself, then flew away—

MARGARET   I know my own poem, Harold.

HAROLD   Then you tell me what's going on.

MARGARET

> From out of the box sailed a flimsy-brimmed hat,
> a red linen hat with two little black ribbons,
> and it fluttered and saucered up high in the rafters.
> then hovered a moment, curtseyed politely,
> and took a full breath of the dust in the attic,
> and sneezed itself into—well, would you believe
> that a hat that can breathe can turn into—a cat?

HAROLD   A cat.

MARGARET   It's the truth. If you doubt it ask Sophie who swears that it happened. "I saw it myself," she will tell you, unless some bad cat's got her tongue.

HAROLD   It all comes down to cats. Again. What else?

MARGARET   I warned you, Harold. What did you expect to dig up in my room? Something incriminating? A Vandalia scandal?

HAROLD   I thought we were through with cats.

MARGARET   There are cats you can't kill.

HAROLD   I just don't get you.

MARGARET   I'm no great mystery.

HAROLD   You are to me.

MARGARET   No more than you are. Do I really know what you did day after day through the years down at the bank—in your meetings, at your conferences in Omaha?

HAROLD   I have been entirely open and public in my life. I never had an upper room. I never disappeared for days at a time.

MARGARET   You disappeared every day. You disappeared into your suit. Into your white collar.

HAROLD   I'm no great mystery. As you would say.

MARGARET   (*From her purse she takes a folded piece of paper.*) No? Who is this?

HAROLD   Who's what?

MARGARET   The name in this letter.

HAROLD   (*Taking the letter out of her hand and glancing at it.*) No one.

MARGARET   You're seventy years old, Harold. There's not enough time left to lie.

HAROLD   It's no one that matters. Not to me.

MARGARET   It's your father.

HAROLD   No, it isn't. You don't know that.

MARGARET   Samuel Kaufman. Sinai Towers. Chicago.

HAROLD   It's not your business.

MARGARET   Ninety-two years old. Frail. Waiting to die. (*HAROLD tears up the letter.*) I have a copy of the letter. I know all about this. I have talked with the company that did your search. And I've talked with the nursing home. And I've talked with Mr. Kaufman.

HAROLD   He's not my father.

MARGARET   He agrees with you on that point. He's not too thrilled with the idea of having a seventy-year-old son in rural Iowa. But from the sound of his tired, halting voice, I'm not sure

what he could get excited about. He says he doesn't know you, but
he did refer to you as "some putz." What's a "putz"?

HAROLD   I think it's Yiddish.

MARGARET   But what is it?

HAROLD   An insult.

MARGARET   What insult?

HAROLD   A penis. What else did he say?

MARGARET   That his son is dead. Ten years ago.

HAROLD   His wife?

MARGARET   Also dead.

HAROLD   Family?

MARGARET   That's pretty hazy. Maybe a daughter. Or a niece. I
couldn't quite make that out. Then I think he put down the phone.
I could hear someone talking in the room. And then I got a dial
tone.

HAROLD   A dial tone. Maybe he died.

MARGARET   No. I sent some flowers. I called the next day, and the
flowers had been delivered.

HAROLD   You know what? He's not your father. Let him die.

MARGARET   He's your father.

HAROLD   No, he's not. You want him? Adopt him.

MARGARET   You find him, and then you turn your back on him.
You were hoping he was dead. You never wanted to find him.

HAROLD   I wanted to know who I was.

MARGARET   You. As usual. Always you. But it doesn't mean any-
thing if you find him and then neglect him. You want to know
who you are? Take a look. What does this tell you about you?

HAROLD   Not much.

MARGARET   You're the diaspora, Harold. In Iowa.

HAROLD   That has nothing to do with me.

MARGARET   How many things can you deny at one time without
being crushed?

HAROLD   I don't have to be anything I don't want to be.

MARGARET   That's right. You're a free man. A free seventy-year-old
man. Behold! It's a miracle! Meanwhile, we're going to Chicago.

HAROLD   No, we're not.

MARGARET   Tell me why.

HAROLD   I don't want to.

MARGARET   Tell me why.

HAROLD   I don't want to see him. I don't want to go into that room and smell the smell and see an old face.

MARGARET   He's right.

HAROLD   What?

MARGARET   You are a putz.

HAROLD   I can't do this. You ask too much.

MARGARET   Well, I'll make you an offer that I'll probably live to regret.

HAROLD   I'm not interested in offers.

MARGARET   Then why did you invite me to dinner? Don't tell me there isn't something you want to negotiate.

HAROLD   Shouldn't we be done with negotiating anything at our age? After half a century together?

MARGARET   We're not there yet.

HAROLD   What's to negotiate?

MARGARET   Are you ready to talk about a proposal?

HAROLD   No. What's your proposal?

MARGARET   I move back home.

HAROLD   I accept.

MARGARET   But it's conditional.

HAROLD   On what?

MARGARET   No more killing. Of anything. Ever.

HAROLD   All right. No more cats.

MARGARET   Not one?

HAROLD   Not one.

MARGARET   Not even one?

HAROLD   One.

MARGARET   Two.

HAROLD   One.

MARGARET   Three.

HAROLD   Two. Neutered. Spayed.

MARGARET   Agreed. Now. Another condition. We go to see your father.

HAROLD   Absolutely not.

MARGARET   How do we get past your fear?

HAROLD   Of? What?

MARGARET   You sleep in the kitchen. You're afraid of my room. You won't visit a harmless old man. You can't set foot inside a nursing home. Have I overlooked anything? Oh, and you shoot harmless cats.

HAROLD   I'm not afraid of cats.

MARGARET   If you're not afraid of dying, then you'll go with me to visit your father.

HAROLD   (*Sitting down at the table.*) I fought in Korea. I saw men die.

MARGARET   Fine. This man is alive.

HAROLD   It's a nursing home. A dead zone.

MARGARET   People live there. And he's your father.

HAROLD   (*Slumping into a chair at the table.*) I don't want to do this.

MARGARET   But you will.

HAROLD   I can't go into that room.

MARGARET   It's a room. We're in a room. (*She walks to stand behind* HAROLD'S *chair, placing her hands on his shoulders.*) It's just a room.

HAROLD   Sooner or later it's the only room. It's not a room to die in.

MARGARET   (*Looking down at* HAROLD *for a long time, then with her hands on his face.*) Why not?
Get out of this hatbox; it isn't a fat box.
There's no room for tabbies who've turned into flabbies,
Whose thin-whiskered hubbies have swelled into tubbies.
(*She reaches down and pats his stomach.*)

HAROLD   (*Holding her hands, but moving them back to his shoulders.*) When we get there, what do we say?

MARGARET   Does it matter? You talk about family. You show pictures. Whatever relatives do.

HAROLD   Why would I want to see him?

MARGARET   You'll see yourself—if you live to ninety-two.

HAROLD   Wonderful! I can watch myself die.

MARGARET   Don't you want that? You get to die without dying. It's the best illusion of all. And you've been trying to find your father for how many years?

HAROLD   I wanted a name. I never intended to see him. I hate family reunions.

MARGARET   I can't believe you wouldn't want to see your own father.

HAROLD   Not this way. Not in the Bedroom of Death. The Bedpan of Death. How can people bear to die that way?

MARGARET   You just wait. And, by the way, this is not some new catastrophe. Every ticking second, for millions of years, this happens to us. All of us.

HAROLD   Not to me it hasn't.

MARGARET

A thin cat named Snippet, a red Abysinnian,
eyes green as olives, dropped down through the dust
to land, as a cat always does, on its feet,
despite having just been a hat sound asleep.

HAROLD   As Sally would say, that's just weird. (*He stands, turns to her, and puts his hands on her waist.*) I hope he doesn't die while we're there.

MARGARET   Let's hope you don't die while we're there.

HAROLD   As the sparks fly upward, I'm a cursed man!

MARGARET   Now, then. What are we going to do about that? Bow our heads? Look away?

CURTAIN

[ENTER GHOST]

1. Retirement's Exile

I taught versions of English for forty-one years and then retired with some ceremony and bon voyage in 2001 from Indiana University South Bend. My wife tells me that I worried over the prospect during the last year in harness, and I remember that we talked about it a lot. She's right, but I don't remember the heights of anxious drama. Fear of psychic free fall in retirement everyone hears about, but no one really knows it till one day near the end we're staring off into space beyond the wall of our offices down into the Grand Canyon. So before we jump or get pushed, the general advice is that we plan some activities to occupy ourselves on the ride down, keeping in mind that activities accelerate time, and plans go awry.

Three months before I retired, I got some bad news, and within two days after I retired, I went to Indianapolis to have surgery for prostate cancer. In the first two years, Cyndi and I vacationed for a month in Rome. We moved twice—to New Buffalo, Michigan, and then to a suburb of Atlanta, and, while Cyndi studied theology at Emory University, I became the Resident Ghost of Hamlet's Father, pacing the parapets of Park Hall in Athens, Georgia.

My psyche was out of breath and ghost-like, nearly invisible. Which is to say that I was teaching part-time—free at last, oh, lord, of tenure, title, private office, fringe benefits, meaningful income, committee memberships, political influence, career friendships, and greetings in hallways and at urinals. Like Saul Bellow's dangling man, at best an attendant adjunct, I carried a heavy freedom. The department at the University of Georgia, uncelebrated for its social warmth, but probably no less hospitable to adjuncts than most other universities, had no interest in the likes of me so long as I met classes and filed syllabi and grades on time. I was a suitable academic; that is, my classroom content and management were uncontroversial. In Michigan, Wyoming, Colorado, and Indiana, no blood had ever flowed into the hallways from under my classroom doors. And so I continued on dazed autopilot for four years in a clean, fluorescent-lighted place.

Maybe it's too much to say that, like Hamlet's murdered father, I was slain by my retirement. And with a teaching schedule and classes to prepare for, I was not in full free fall. It helped that Cyndi swam the arterial currents of commuter traffic into Atlanta several days a week. Institutions that expect us to show up at scheduled times drum a little rhythm into the seven days.

Before my prose shuffles off to shine a light on more ordinary ghosts and other has-beens, here's one more grandiose Shakespearian parallel to latter-day retirement: Lear gave his kingdom away to two of his daughters and tried desperately to live on with an entourage and some kingly authority; then, driven by pride and unloving daughters, he wandered onto the stormy heath to huddle with Poor-Tom's-a-Cold. The caution in the tale: unless we retire with considerable wealth to maintain a kind of shadow after-kingdom, we will be like Lear, uncrowned, unconsulted, denied.

But in Lear's kingdom he had no Huddle House to huddle in. In my retirement, my father-in-law and I went out to breakfast once a week. We started with a Waffle House (see ubiquitous yellow signs in Georgia). Before we upgraded to IHOP, we had become familiars of an elderly waitress. She was efficient and pretty attentive, and, before Christmas, festive:

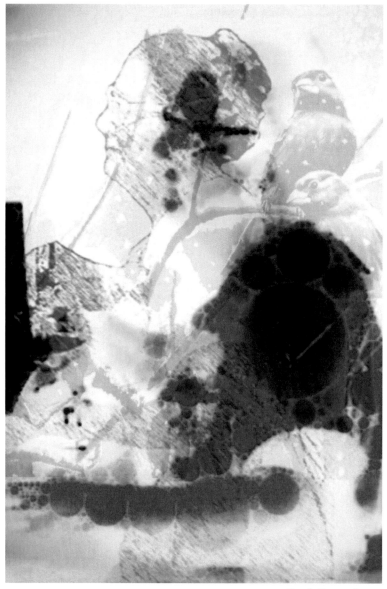

Sandy Brown Jensen

Stars in Her Hair

A few years ago, Ebb and I sat down
to breakfast at a Waffle House
in Buford amid the usual din and drift
of coffee, waffles, eggs, and grits.

One morning a cook hadn't shown up,
and our waitress, hovering around seventy-five,
the one we hoped to see every Christmas,
told us, when we asked for more coffee,
"Now look, boys, I can't do everything."

But today the whole shift comes in. Maybe
she remembers us; she calls Ebb "Honey."
We tally who gets more affection:
Hon, Honey, Darlin', Baby, Sweetie.
We agree on "Darlin'" as most intimate.

She works at Waffle House because she has to,
for a few dollars an hour and tips, and here
she is again, in her Santa sweater.
Her blond hair, dyed, curled, sprayed,
sprinkled with blue, red, silver and gold, glimmers
under a net of tiny Christmas lights
she wears on her head to work every year.

"Your lights are out," we tell her. "Boys,
they were on when I came in this morning."
She pats the battery pack beneath
her sweater, the stars twinkle on,
and people set their forks down to applaud.

Better to pat the battery pack than to curse the darkness.

Besides those who can't afford to retire from their jobs, a huge geriatric population is at work across the land in various on-your-feet-for-hours, low-paid service jobs. The first job during high school for some turns out to be the last job in retirement for others. There they are, peeling open and packing plastic sacks, wearing the grocery store T-shirt stamped Publix, Krogers, Ingles, Safeway, or Winn-Dixie, offering to help me wheel the cart to the car. I never let anyone help me with my cart—yet. But to these old guys, some of them older than I am, shuffling a little, a little stooped, maybe embarrassed that they need to do this to pay the bills, to these guys I should be saying, "Come on, dump this sorrowful job. Let's go up to the Waffle House in Buford. There's someone I want you to meet."

For some of us elderly, taking a part-time job is a kind of unfelonious recidivism. Even when we qualify for Social Security and a pension, a lifetime of habitual employment persists. Some of us can't not work—until we can't work anymore. Work is a place to go, with a schedule that names the otherwise nameless days of newspapers, television, restaurants of comfort food, walking and being walked by the dog, and doctors' appointments.

Even retired prehistoric homo sapiens must have grown tired of staring at cave paintings of bison and deer and got out of the cave from time to time. Muscle fibers get restless, joints stiffen, and the imagination needs motion and alternatives. The spirit needs to flex.

Or it will get flexed. James Ray Roney in Cowarts, Alabama, retired from selling insurance and didn't know what to do with himself, so he began advising his wife on how to cook and clean house, which advice she had not needed during the previous half-century. Finally she showed him the open door to the rest of the world, saying, "This house is mine to manage. All the rest out there—that's yours." So he began delivering prescriptions for the Wiregrass Pharmacy, arriving every morning to make coffee and small talk and to exercise his folk humor, which he was good at. He knew better than to advise the pharmacists.

But there comes a time when the brain's curiosity gradually turns passive. Amazement turns to dazed waiting. Growing up in the '40s, for me the best show in Detroit was at the zoo at the Jo Mendi chimpanzee circus. The intelligence and curiosity of chimpanzees led to their being trained to ride bicycles, walk on their hands, wear costumes, and generally behave conspicuously like the close relatives to humans that they are. At 74, entering the falling-down-years, I wish I had their long arms and short legs so I could knuckle-walk. The chimps in the Jo Mendi ensemble that followed him out of the 1930s, if they lived long enough, lost their ability to interact and perform, and lapsed into retirement, sitting without audience in their stalls, sullen and abstracted, waiting into nothing:

> And, nothing himself, beholds
> Nothing that is not there and the nothing that is.
> —*Wallace Stevens,* "The Snow Man"

Those of us who don't succumb to disease or catastrophe earlier in life can look forward to some version of the diminished life. Our shrinking brains (by the way, chimpanzees' brains don't shrink), our atrophying muscle mass, our calcium-starved skeletons, and our gravity-sagged bags of skin work steadily behind and on the scenes of Act V.

Meanwhile, we have to flex ourselves. Get out the guitar or plug in the electrical piano. I recommend headphones so others don't have to listen until we're concert-ready, which will be never. Or grow an herb garden indoors to have fresh basil, parsley, and rosemary through the winter freezes. Weekly watering helps to mark the passing of time. Study a foreign language and find someone in town who will speak it with you. Start with Spanish for the most opportunities; Italian and Portugese are then in reach. Watch French and German language films with subtitles on Netflix. "Okay" and "No problem" work in all languages.

Nevertheless, our range of flex inexorably narrows. Poet Donald Hall at 83 writes of easy chair vigils from his family home in New Hampshire. "Whatever the season, I watch the barn. . . . Over eighty years it has changed from a working barn to a barn for looking at. . . . Out the window, I watch a white landscape that turns pale green, dark green, yellow and red, brown under bare branches, until snow falls again." From a working poet, Hall has changed to a man looking—at a barn. He writes that the metaphors no longer come to him for poems, but he continues to write the prose of elderly solitude, an exiled witness to his surrounding farm.

The predicament of exile begins when consciousness begins to watch itself from what must have seemed another place, not knowing who was dreaming and watching. Traveling through sleep and memory. Waking on the limb of a tree. Being and the thought of being clinging to each other like monkeys, the eons unfurling their double lives.

How do we separate the idea of self-awareness from our narratives of consciousness, our story-making spirit? Before humans began to think about it as consciousness, there was consciousness. Pre-histories imagined on glaciers under starlight. Stories and dreams in restless sleep. When the cave painters at Chauvet moved their fingers across stones, did they watch themselves painting? Did they believe another being was painting through them, moving beneath their hands? Divinities or demons. Spirits of the dead riding the grave bison and the listening ibex. That was 30,000 years ago, and we have only now met ourselves in the ancient caves of wonderment.

THE WIG ON THE BEACH

Not a bald head in sight, only hair sewn
to a thin skull of net, full curls good enough to run
to the drugstore or to sign for the delivery truck.
Had any boats gone down in the storm
that tore all night at the ragged coast?
Did she jump? Could he swim?
Experts may take years to trace
the label, analyze the residue
of hand lotion, construct a jaw line
and eye sockets, scrape and brush for shards
of cookery, knives of ritual sacrifice, guess
how a beach might grow a cheap wig
that could think, headless,
awash on the blowing sand:

Filaments of northwest wind spin the sand
into fibers, swirl crystals into hair which flutters
in the wind; like spiders, it begins to walk
into the grass, graze. The same wind hollows
a rock into a skull, gusts, buffets the skull
into a first ache of learning, which becomes
the first wig of consciousness beside the blank,
untraveled water; early homo sapiens gazes
on the morning, how the first light grows
yellow on the wave crests, breaks down
in the shallows, blue, running over green stones.

Time rises out of dying, grows
out of remembering. What time is it now?
the wig asks, does not remember
that she had asked what time it was
in a prior space where she wore someone's head,

not remembering that she could not remember
she was dying and so she curled
into her pillow like the cat on the pillow itself.

The swimmers will not wear wigs in the afternoon.
Wide-eyed in their masks among the imaginary fish
eating on the exquisite reef, they grin
around their mouthpieces at the green
and yellow and blue of the parrot fish. For once
they are not afraid. Or bored. Later they will climb
out of the surf into the great bulk of their shoulders
and bellies, stumble ashore to the exile of paragraphs
and questions. They will try not to sleep it all off.

Blue clouds slide down the horizon
over the gray water, their fine blue hair
slanting long on the wind. A wig
sees hair everywhere, even in the rain.
A wig wants something to ride and someone
to talk, which is why stories report
conversation, as if all that sand
were not enough to start a wig thinking
about things such as love and the need for death,
something to feed the hungry shore.
And all that water always sinking in,
all that water. Waves falling into foam, crumble
into rotten marble, dissipate to glass, shatter.
She knew of two reasons for dying:
the failure of memory and the loss of wonderment.
She knew that love at times had buried each.

In the 1940s, I began to notice me noticing me but only vaguely sensed it as an aura out of which I would begin to tell me about myself in stories. This is one such story—about stories. It didn't occur to me then that others might be so self-absorbed. It didn't occur to me then that this was the beginning of exile, the first separation from self that displaces us from full presence in the acting moment. Wordsworth romanticized it as a withdrawal from the oversoul.

All our cries to seize the day, to live wholly in the holy moment, cry against the exile of self-knowing that divides us from ourselves. To be human is to live in exile, and our yearning to rise out of ourselves into the lap of god or the arms of a lover or to make a long pilgrimage out of time or into history flies to and from that boundless exile.

Billy Bigelow, the hapless carnival barker in *Carousel*, stands with Julie Jordan under a night sky on the coast of Maine, unable to simply sing that he loves her, only "if I loved you." "Look up there. What are we? Just a couple o' specks o' nothin'." That moment catches the contradictory sense of our insignificant insignificance, after which he bungles his ambitions mortally in a failed robbery attempt to "provide" for their unborn child. Billy has only a glimmer of what we are now told is a universe of 100 sextillion stars, and three times that in a recent postulation.

Whether there are 100 sextillion stars, or 300 sextillion stars, the implications for humans on earth and their place in the universe are vast, not to mention incomprehensible. The centrality of the human predicament in the universe seems to shrivel like a raisin.

It doesn't occur to me in 1956 as I'm watching that movie in a Detroit theatre that I'm at least as inept and insignificant as Billy. Human history and the disinterested cosmos don't blink at a guy who drops out of college in the spring of his freshman year. On State Street in Ann Arbor, I had watched the Sigma Chi float go by. One of my dorm roommates, a fraternity pledge, is flat on his back inside the float, wagging a large bunny ear. He's drunk; I'm making another senseless, early exit.

But I'm not going to drape the exit in some illusion of chronology and causal sequence. Now when I seem to remember that parade and movie, do I remember the events themselves or my remembered, massaged narratives of the events?

Fifty years later, we're waiting for another parade on the side of gravel Highway 34 in Costa Rica. Cyndi and I wait for a bus in Matapalo, a little pueblo on the Pacific, where the tiniest pulperias call themselves mini-super-mercados, and electricity is too expensive to turn on the lights. Surrounding the dusty buses are schedules and schedule rumors. Nothing printed. Only oral reports.

We listen to la lluvia falling, beating down the dust, which it does part of most days during the green season. Mist builds to rain clouds in the afternoons, veiling the mountains at our back, then dropping its torrential curtain around two o'clock.

About twenty miles south in Dominical, fifty minutes down the rock-crusted road in 2007, there's a farmacia where we'll pick up some medications and practice our Spanish—if we can catch a bus. No one we talk to seems to know the schedule. Pronto. Luego. People gather around the benches during the morning. No one looks up the road. There's no anticipation.

Two days we wait nearly an hour. Twice we miss the afternoon return bus from Dominical. The first day we find a taxi (twelve thousand colones = twenty-four dollars). Our very kind driver is amazed that his name in the U.S. would be Rudolph. Another day, all the taxis have left, apparently for San Isidro in the mountains.

Godot never comes to Costa Rica; he already came. Here it's "*ya pasado,*" as one gentle Costa Rican woman tells me when I ask what time the bus leaves to return to Matapalo. *Ya pasado.* Already passed. The next bus? *Mañana por la mañana.* Tomorrow morning. Everything has already happened here along the ocean's edge, under the falling mangoes, the whirring hummingbirds, the skittering ctenosaurs. With gin on the balcony in the leather-backed rocking chairs, we swoon in the now and all. Even mañana seems over. *Ya pasado.*

In his late years, Mark Twain said that his memory had declined, that when he was younger he could remember everything, whether it happened or not. The rest of us think we remember our childhoods clearly and accurately, and we describe them sometimes in relentless detail. Interrupting elders' stories to say that you know the stories only delays the inevitable. They will resume to the finish. My mother, growing up in Holland, Michigan, had to learn to drive the family car in 1920 because her father, a blacksmith, despised motorized vehicles. She was sixteen. My wife's father in 1935 drove a team of mules through the starry Alabama night with a wagonload of cotton bound for the gin. He was ten.

As much as we the elderly burden those around us with good-old-days human interest stories, and with our infirmities and forgetfulness, we're not without our usefulness. Some services we provide unknowingly, as I came to learn over years of teaching.

A TRIBUTE TO GRANDPARENTS
(*Indiana University Alumni Magazine*, 1991)

I want to say a few words to grandparents everywhere, and especially to the grandparents of students at Indiana University South Bend, about whom I know the most and to whom I address this speech in tribute and gratitude. Even in astonishment. Each year the Society for Unsung Heroes recognizes unusual achievement in selfless service. Before I announce this year's hero, I'll tell you the story behind it.

The support that makes education possible for students at IUSB has countless members—parents, spouses, brothers and sisters, friends and lovers, employees who allow flexible work schedules, and grandparents. Yes, the grandparents who die many times before their deaths. You have given not only your genes, your advice, and sometimes your financial assistance, but you have often made the supreme sacrifice of life itself, that your grandchildren might hand in a term paper late without penalty. You give of yourselves without recognition and without reward. Sometimes you don't know yourselves what you have done.

Three years ago, a student called my office to say that she could not take the mid-term exam in American Literature. Jessica told me that her grandmother had passed away the day before. The sound of sorrow filled her voice as she struggled to keep her composure. I asked whether the passing had been unexpected.

"You mean like did we think she would never die?"

"No," I said, soothingly. Jessica was silent for a long moment.

"Had you been close to your grandmother?"

"You know, I never knew Grandma that well. She lived in Duluth. But Mom is having a hard time. They were very close. I'm just glad I can be here for her. I try to put on a happy face—even when my heart's not in it."

I reassured Jessica that however great the grief of the moment, sorrow works its way through. She said that she would try to remember my advice over the long drive to Des Moines.

Poor child! She was, no doubt, in some form of denial. Her grandmother was lying in state in Duluth, and here was Jessica heading for Iowa. "Duluth," I reminded her. "Duluth." Organ music rising in the background, Jessica began to cry rhythmically, so I wished her the best and told her to contact me about a make-up exam as soon as she felt up to it.

About a year later, I happened to see Jessica at the Oaken Bucket, reading a book while she ate. I waved to her, but she looked troubled, so I went over to say hello. She was unable to concentrate on either her novel or her cheeseburger because her grandfather in Detroit had just died. I asked whether he was the widower of the grandmother she had lost, as I recalled, a year ago.

"Almost to the day," she said, "just like we learned in psychology class, you know, how the elderly tend to hang on until anniversaries and birthdays?"

"And mid-term exams," I observed, but Jessica again was silent, lost in some meditation on mortality. "Didn't your grandmother live in Duluth?" Jessica gave me what might have been a look of reproach.

"Yes, she did, but Duluth had too many memories, so Granddaddy had to go live with his sister in Dubuque."

So many deaths, I thought. So many cities that begin with D.

Here, then, is the remarkable part of the story. A few months later Jessica's Grandma Evelyn died again—during final exams—in a fall from a rooftop, this time in DeKalb, where she had taken a job as a part-time chimney sweep to supplement her meager Social Security check, never telling her loved ones how great her need had been.

What pleases me to share with you is the good news that, however many times they may die, and Grandma Evelyn has passed on, or, should I say, has recycled, a total of seven times, grandparents do recover and resume their lives. If ever there were an argument for life after death, even for reincarnation—well, I could write a book.

You grandparents, it turns out, have more lives than the neighbor's cat. You may suffer injury, you may suffer long illness, and you may die at inconvenient times, but you will live to die again. You may not be immortal, but so long as you have grandchildren in college, you will live. And you will be of continual service to your grandchildren in the timeliness of your passing and in your good judgment always to die out of town without benefit of local obituary.

Tonight's Unsung Hero Award goes to Evelyn Penmark, the grandmother of Jessica Penmark, a senior theatre major. Jessica and her grandparents are unable to be here tonight to receive the award. Jessica does, however, send her regrets and asks your sympathy and understanding in her hour of grief.

Postscript

Twenty-one years after writing that speech, I hope that I'll serve often as a mourned grandparent, maybe for Tory Vander Ven now at Ohio University, or later for the other three grandchildren. We should write our obituaries now and give copies to the grandchildren with the advice: *change date and other details as needed. Familiarize yourself with the obituary. You may be questioned.*

While serving humbly, a lot of us geezers persist in breathing the pleasures of life as seasonal refugees, taking cruises and other trips, or moving south to Purgatory, Florida, or Limbo, Arizona. We ruefully declare that the bad news of the far future doesn't apply. Global warming, rising seas, and fossil fuel depletion are somebody else's problem (read "great-grandchildren"). Tell them to buy property about 50 feet above sea level for their eventual retirement beach home, when Florida becomes the new Atlantis. Inland from Brunswick, Georgia (elevation, 10 ft.), Nahunta (elevation, 66 ft., population, 930), may be the next retirement resort, though I haven't been there to count the Confederate battle flags.

Companion of self-awareness and equally problematic is our awareness of our deaths. Much of our lives we spend justifying our existence with elaborate projects and mission statements—careers, conquests, hobbies, and fantasies. Some of the effort goes to making our unbearable lightness of being bearable, and some of it goes to redefining our deaths as not deaths as all, but as passages to new and eternal lives, preferably stress-free and in good company.

Retirement and migration serve some of us as a practice run, a prelude to the after-life's eternal community activities building. Morning coffee, Internet news, and sudoku in a lanai beside a canal in Naples, Florida. Or spandex-bicycling to a market in Sun City, Arizona for vegetables—in an effort to postpone becoming one. For some of us, the only service we offer humanity in the latter-day leisure years is surrendering our car keys before we drift onto the shoulder or across a median or pull out into traffic and take out an entire family.

But what makes us think we deserve to retire? The natural world—with its cycles of drought, flood, storm, famine, and the periodic exhaustion (see Easter Island) of resources such as fuel—really doesn't care if we retire or work till we can't stagger to our feet anymore. The entropy of aging tells us it would be very good not to have to work, or at least to labor at a slower pace, for shorter hours, and on a schedule of our choosing. But beyond that, retirement as a social institution is no more than that—a cultural value made possible by economics, government programs, family husbandry, and dumb luck. The belief that we've worked "long enough and hard enough" that we deserve not to work anymore is no more than a cultural construction.

Not that we should cancel our retirement plans if we can afford to stop working and live the life of a sloth without enervating guilt. And rationalizing has gotten us where we are; why not keep it up as best we can? Rationalizing is practically on autopilot by the time we retire. That, combined with the steady and inexorable decline of energy and stamina, guides us onto a glide path of semi-supine and sponge-like waiting, for which 20th century technology has prepared us well:

John S. DeFord

STATE OF RECLINERY

Please help me. I can't get out of my recliner. But I'm not going to buy one of those electric chairs that boosts me to my feet. Maybe it's only an urban legend that a guy in Des Moines pushed the lift button and got catapulted through his picture window into the front yard. Still, should I buy a recliner that's been endorsed by a test pilot?

Market showrooms are full of Toyota-Hyundai-Chevy recliners, but no mass-production chair meets everyone's needs. You may have to choose a boutique product: a Toledo Mud Hens recliner, a Unitarian-Universalist recliner, a Gershwin medley recliner, or a mission-style recliner (John Muir autograph model). I wanted to buy a Zen Recliner, but my wife cited my history of falling asleep and running off the road while en route to satori.

So I ended up buying a Scandinavian model. When you tip back all the way, it eliminates gravitational pressure. Your spine feels like mashed potatoes. If you're in your living room, and you're a product of Western Culture, this chair is probably as close to levitation as you're going to get.

It's the perfect lift-off position, but only if you're on a launch pad heading into orbit. Getting upright to exit the chair requires a particular combination of upper-body muscles that you never needed in your entire life until you reclined in this chair. Of course, there's no instructional DVD in the show room that tells you about the eight-week conditioning program and the personal trainer you'll need in order to tilt back and later on escape. Who's going to buy THAT chair? Who's going to buy a recliner with a warning tag, "Women: do not try this at home unless attended by another adult"?

A lot of recliners look like giant bran muffins. You probably have one. It's designed so that when you sit down you have no fear of injury. The only things missing are a seat belt and an airbag. A rear-end collision will have to get through the wall behind you before impact, reducing the force by a factor of seven. And front-end collisions? There is no record of a reclined person ever being physically injured by a television program, a magazine, or a nap. Gazing up into Internet space through the window of an iPad or a Kindle when getting sleepy is another matter. Check the bridge of my nose the next time we meet in the produce section.

Recliners, like muffins, do come with a variety of fruity and nutty features. Rockers. Swivels. Vibrators. None of which compromise the spirit of reclination. The recliner, like Lebowski, abides. You can swivel and rock and vibrate all at the same time, but you're still reclining in Knoxville. That's why out-of-shape recliner vaqueros keep climbing back into the saddle. It never leaves the corral.

There are, however, some accessories that do not, in my opinion, abide. For example, the black plastic beer can holder built into armrests. It lowers property values. It's a black hole in the universe of reclination—from which you cannot escape with dignity. Likewise with built-in radios, mini-refrigerators, and PEZ dispensers. Users may apply for an exemption for a remote control storage space, provided the space has an understated, preferably invisible, lid. A recliner should always look like a recliner—not like a dentist's chair.

And the Siamese double recliner also violates the rich spirit of reclination, meditation, and individuation that embraces America.

The art of naming has itself become problematic. Take, for example, the Simmons Truffle Micro Fiber Fabric Massage Recliner with Cup Holder. Should I eat it? Smoke it? Ask it out for coffee? I'm holding out till that model includes an ATM. A lot of credit has to go to the two Eds who settled on the warm, fuzzy self-deprecating name, La-Z-Boy. The Wikipedia recliner site reports, "The 'La-Z-Boy' name came about as the result of a fat employee being lazy and skipping work," but a Wiki warning says that this information may be a hoax. Even if the story is true, it diminishes the brilliance of the name, which anticipates the great classic celebration of laziness, "Lazy Bones," the Johnny Mercer and Hoagy Carmichael song of 1933. They probably wrote it in a recliner.

A friendly companion to the possibly apocryphal La-Z-Bones story is this item of Americana. The BarcaLounger Company, La-Z-Boy's rival in recliner manufacturing, "is reputed to be the first American company to allow its employees coffee breaks, in 1902" (followed by the familiar Wiki alert, "citation needed"). Only in America!

For People In Later Life, the recliner is the second most important item in the house (the top-rated item will be discussed in another column, once we get to know each other better). Some PILLs use their recliner for nearly everything—meals, naps, television viewing, reading, naps, crossword puzzles, phone conversations, naps, and, if they have laptops, as an Internet station. These (with minor variants) account for virtually all known sedentary activities.

But how did Western society get from the 19th-century fainting couch on which women in corsets collapsed to the post-WWII recliner on which fat guys collapsed? The demise of the fainting couch has been attributed to the passage of the constitutional amendment guaranteeing women the right to breathe. The advent of the recliner appears to have been made possible by the shortening of the work-day and the workweek. Guys have been granted more leisure time in which to gain weight and to watch television. By the 1950s, Western men and women no longer had to go to the bedroom to lie down. The recliner became a designated safe zone for idleness and shameless snoring in the midst of living room traffic. It's a bed masquerading as a chair.

Furniture designers after the turn of the century had begun to realize that a society that enabled people to work fewer hours and have more unproductive, leisure time needed a way to take pressure off the spine and elevate the legs. In Monroe, Michigan, in the 1920s, cousins Edward Knabusch and Edwin Shoemaker were inventors. Since Edison and Bell had already come up with the light bulb and the phone, they sat around for long hours in that Bethlehem of invention, the garage, trying to come up with the next transformative technology.

Ed looks at Ed, who's sitting on a wooden chair with his feet on an orange crate and complaining about a sore back and tired legs. Light bulb goes on. Bell rings. A chair that tilts backward and elevates the feet. Within days, they assemble the raw-pine prototype. A company buyer, his name lost to history, drops by the garage and, after a short nap, says, hey, why don't you use cushions?

During this era, engineers and inventors were pursuing two seemingly unrelated research paths that converged dramatically on the night of October 15, 1951, when viewers all over America leaned back in their recliners and watched the first episode of *I Love Lucy*. That night we now recognize as a high-water mark of civilization.

But now looms the deeper question of reclination: what does it really mean to recline? Both the chair itself and the person in it are recliners, woven together, melded, joined like Siamese twins. You know the feeling. Of the two common meanings of reclination, "the act of leaning or reclining, or the state of being reclined," let's go with the former meaning, reclination as an active process, rather than as a passive state to which no one will admit. Has anyone ever answered the phone and said, "I was asleep in my recliner when you called"?

Okay. Appearances deceive. A person reclining seems to be passively sleeping, possibly soul-crooning, but may, in fact, be actively solving a difficult math problem: Roger spends 23 hours per week watching NBA basketball and averages one beer per hour. How many pounds of pretzels will he consume by the time Carmelo Anthony retires?

Or maybe the left brain is at work. Bob is both reclining and ascending to a spiritual state bordering nirvana, neither suffering nor desiring. Whether he can achieve transcendence while watching a bass fishing tournament is still in clinical studies.

Which somehow leads to the question of the side effects of recliners. Not just small side effects on you, but giant contraindications for mankind. Research would suggest that environmentalist warnings about the contribution of recliner flatulence to global warming appear to be unwarranted. Yes, clouds of methane do rise intermittently from some recliners, but only two-thirds of humans actually produce methane when they fart. Further, there is no evidence that flatulence is higher in men than in women or that recliners are the cause of a net volume increase in flatulence. (For an in-depth discussion of flatulence, see http://www.heptune.com/farts.html.)

If you're in your recliner while reading this article—and YOU SHOULD BE—be generous. Consider yourself in an active state of reclination. Socrates, if he were alive and would stop saying things like "the truth is, O men of Athens, . . . that the wisdom of men is little or nothing," then we could all take a nap, without the aid of hemlock. When he was on his game, he said things with more practical applications, such as, and I paraphrase, "The unexamined recliner is not worth sleeping in."

Yeats agreed with Socrates: a man in a recliner who neither reasons nor reflects is "but a paltry thing, / A tattered coat upon a stick. . . ." If you merely snooze when you're not neurotically changing channels, if you don't remember the next day whether you finished the article on renewable energy, then you are reclining—may I say it?—irresponsibly, without regard for the sort of planet you will leave behind for your grandchildren to recline on.

But if you have found at times that after entering reclination for a period of time that you, not just your spine, but you in your supine profundity have loosed the bonds of lunch, sports, yard work, and the urge to get another dog, then you have at last achieved a *state of reclinery.*

They can't take that away from you.

Planet Tithonus

It's the planet of your descendants, if earth continues to be inhabitable. All the medical progress, particularly in genetic research and engineering, leads to something like the state of life on the Planet Tithonus, in the galaxy M31, Andromeda. PT was first detected when the space explorer, Infinitum, approached and began sending back photos and measurements in 2003. Slightly larger than earth, and with a daily rotation of 27 earth hours and an annual orbit around its star, Begorrah, of 485 earth days, Planet Tithonus turns out to give us an odd window into a possible future for homo sapiens. Infinitum's landing vehicle spent six weeks on the surface of PT, recording video and collecting and analyzing samples of soil and water. Only in the last week did robots detect that the large, green plants with hairy fronds that waved in the strong, prevailing breezes of PT, were not plants after all. Rather, they were once mobile (tri-pedal) organisms of a social species that had developed history and culture, and eventually spun its self-knowledge and technology into regrettable advances, verging on immortality.

Okay, it's true that there's a galaxy, M31, also called Andromeda (one trillion stars), but the rest of that story is bunk. What did happen is that we recently spent a few weeks in Tithonia on the Alabama Gulf Coast, where I met and interviewed some people who appear to be living out a very long, leisurely, coastal life—leisurely, at least until the planet's seas rise, and they have to pack up and retreat upland towards Montgomery. This community should not be confused with the Tithonia Civilization data, for which see: marsanomalyresearch. com/evidence-reports/2005/081/tithonia-civilization.htm.

Tithonia, Alabama, is a beach village of about 3,000 extraordinarily aged humanoid beings. Its sister site is Shambhala in Central Asia. Really, Shambhala is better understood as a kingdom, but its population is so small (200,000) spread over vast grasslands that Tithonia and Shambhala adopted each other, in effect, girdling the earth with their spiritual and workout energy. And, since some Shambhalaian people two thousand years ago worshipped the sun, Tithonians feel a kinship in their modern devotion to nature, outdoor exercise, tanning, and leather goods.

Shambhalaians seek spiritual wholeness and oneness with the cosmos. Tithonians seek physical wholeness and longevity, or oneness with themselves in the pursuit of healthy elder bodies. For the people of Shambhala, life is a preparation for reentry in a higher state of being. For most people of Tithonia, the contemplation of this life's end, that is, death, is counter-productive and defeatist. They believe that when they confront their mortality, they begin to decompose right in front of the mirror, which surrender is okay if you live in White Flag, Idaho, but not here on the palmy verge of the tropics.

Of what possible use is it to think about our eventual moment of death? Most thinking is about the events that lead to death and about what, if anything, comes after death for the individual consciousness. We also explore—with faith, skepticism, or disbelief—the relationship between the before and the possible after. Emily Dickinson imagines that the narrator of a poem "heard a fly buzz when I died," and then

"I could not see to see." Even that moment is the final moment of the senses, before death itself. We also hear from those who seem to die on the operating table and then return to report on what some believe is a post-death consciousness and even a perception of the material world from a position outside the body. They say that they witnessed themselves and, for example, the operating room from outside their bodies, implying that they were a hovering spirit with both consciousness and the power to see independent of the body's eyes and optic nerves. Enter ghost. Then exit back into the body.

We have, understandably, no witnesses to the end of consciousness itself, that is, a state of oblivious post-consciousness. And the absence of "evidence" for oblivion frees us to occupy that state with everything from horrific, eternal wailing of punished souls to eternal joyful celebration of rewarded souls. Some merely imagine departed loved ones laughing and playing cards in a kind of celestial retirement facility.

Belief in afterlife isn't really disputable, though some versions of heaven strike me as implausible, particularly ones that people imagine as familiar, comfortable risk-free worlds of old friends and dear relatives, absent of change, anticipation, uncertainty, problems and problem-solving, competition, reproduction, pain and death. Without politics, economics, and gossip. In short, nothing to do. Nothing to wonder about. Nothing to hope for since all is fulfilled. Like Christmas morning after all the presents have been unwrapped.

Imagine having consciousness without a sense of the future. In this world, that may be the state of the profoundly and interminably depressed, leading to suicide.

I seem incapable of imagining my conscious self after death in any form that is in some sense me. How very Anglo-Saxon! Flying in and out of the mead hall between darknesses. Cyndi holds out hope that I will yet find faith before I die. No, she believes that I will. And I love her for that, among so many other things. But most of the time I'm the guy from Maine who's been asked directions. "You can't get there from here." From time to time, I try to imagine what it would be like to believe in the good, brave Christ as a divine and resurrected sacrifice. But that's as far as I get—trying to imagine.

Meanwhile, we go about the work of aging, that is, those of us who get to live long lives. Many years ago, my brother Ned, who will be eighty this summer, said, though he never lived on a farm, that he hoped when he became mentally dysfunctional in old age that someone would take him out behind the barn and put a bullet in his brain. And there's my eighty-seven-year-old father-in-law, whose weapon of choice in recent years, he will say with a smile, is an ax. Like a mule that has come up lame. And that's about as much wishful, ineffectual planning as most of us can manage. And then one morning we wake up old.

At the nursing home, the staff wrote my mother's name on her walker with a marker pen but left a gap between the "Rut" and the "h." She asked me what "Rut h" meant. She moved slowly past the mirror in her room. In her early eighties, despite her dementia, she had moments of a kind of clarity. She turned to the mirror and after a moment recognized herself as though she had not seen her image for a very long time. "When did I get so old?" When indeed? All our illusory narratives of time and ambition can't prepare us for the figure in the mirror—shorter, stooped, its face grooved and sagging, its hair, thinned and white.

from the mirror
of my mother
a great exhale
of stories

STONE CORNER

In the morning light I woke to a diaphonous breath, not mine nor anyone's in the room, like the last breathing in of my mother's lungs, but something with the volume of a cloud. In a naked crouch at the window, I saw on the school playground across the street a gas burner blowing hot air into a striped balloon the size of a house. I shivered as it rose into the morning sky beyond the budding April trees.

Back in bed, I wound through the orchards of October in southwestern Michigan, driving southward, back to Indiana, my mother's ashes in the passenger seat. On the hills among the vineyards north of Berrien Springs, I heard her breathing hard on her last day, feverish with pneumonia. Pulling off onto the gravel shoulder, I turned off the engine. While her lungs and heart fought to carry oxygen to her cells, little spoons of ice cream melted at the back of her throat, pooling till she swallowed. Over the long rows of grapevines beyond a stand of trees, a great balloon, red and yellow, round and rising, lifted a basket of wickering souls upward into the cloudless air.

I imagined my mother having the ride of her after-life. I often tried to remember who she had been before the oxygen supply to her brain waned, before her mind had to reinvent itself among the severed moments in the nursing home, where things slipped away and became other things. Most of the time her clock was not a clock. She would tried to turn it on like a radio, biting her lower lip, turning her face to the wall. Usually the ritual occurred in the morning, part of her routine disorientation. She grasped for someone to blame, usually me because I lived in South Bend and saw her regularly, but she could not think how I got away with it.

Sometimes the numbers on the clock were not numbers. Through the middle lens of her trifocals she would count four red segments in the number four, three vertical and one horizontal. The five had five segments, two horizontal. The six had six segments, three horizontal. But the one had two, the three had five, the seven three.

Ed Brandt

One day she wrote all this down as if it might be a code to break. Notes and letters she stuffed into the drawer of her nightstand and into the pockets of her clothes. "Dear Mom and Dad, please come and get me. They won't let me out. Stuart has hidden my money. He tricked me into coming to live in this hell hole. Love, Ruth." Through the long day the clock digited up the minutes while she waited for her mother and father to appear in the doorway to carry her home to childhood.

Sometimes when she called me Stuart, I would tried to correct her genealogy, but my version was a corrupt weave of Dr. Seuss, the King James Book of Genesis, and the lineage of a dog: "Mom, Sam I am not. Tom I am. I am not your husband. Try to remember that Samuel begat Emanuel out of Spaniel. It is written." No wonder she didn't trust me.

She looked out from her digiting space to tell me the daily news: "Jeanette and Tedd stopped by this morning," and I, who a few months ago would have said, "Jeanette and Tedd are dead," said, instead, "Well, that was nice of them to stop by," and add for my own wan amusement, "Are they still here?" She would scowl at me but forget why because each minute told her only the story of itself.

In each measure of footsteps along the hallway my mother heard the story of Uncle Martin, leaving to cure his tuberculosis in Colorado, who became in the doorway a chaplain of no denomination full of every good wish, smiling his face into Mr. Harrington from the corner of 10th Street in Holland, asking after her mother, who, if it were 1947, would be dying of cancer. Other steps would pass away to other rooms.

"Would you like to come home with me for dinner on Sunday?" I'd ask, half-heartedly. I'd staged a Christmas for her two years before, trying to keep her attention while I fixed a meal, but she was a tough audience, rocking and fussing in the living room by the fireplace, a green throw over her legs, while the annual WFMT airing of "A Child's Christmas in Wales" vexed her nervous system.

I baked a ham, stabbed full of cloves, slick in its own fat. I had found cloth napkins, green ones, and in the back of a kitchen drawer jammed full of debris, red candles.

"Stuart!" she called. "Stuart?"

"I'm in the dining room. We're about ready to eat."

"I think I have to use the bathroom."

"Can you hold on for a minute?"

"I'm afraid I'm going to have an accident."

A train derailment, a truck collision, a fuel spill, and fire engines. Helping her make the slow walk with her walker, I grew angry with myself for my pointless anger with her. Think life cycle, I told myself. Think human history. Pre-history. Think Mary Leakey, finding Ruth Hoekstra's beginnings. The fax reads: Fly Kenya at once. Growing evidence your mother Ruthie here 3.4 million years ago. Bring cast of footprints. Tell no one.

On the way back from the bathroom, she announced that she was ready to go home.

"But we're just sitting down to dinner. It's Christmas, Mom."

"I know that. But we should be starting for home. I don't like being away so long."

"So tell me, Mom, how long do you think you've been here?"

"Oh, I don't know, but I suppose you do." She sounded trapped, as if I had found out how little she knew about anything. "Don't think I'm not on to you. Don't think you can fool me."

"There is no Santa now, is there?" At fifty-one, four years from my own AARP card, I was smart-assing my eighty-four-year-old mother while I served the dowager queen.

I got her to sit down to dinner, but she ate almost nothing, pushing the food around her plate between sips from a water glass that trembled in her hand. She was her own earthquake. The fourth time she said she needed to get home, I gave up on the dinner and drove her back to Evening Dale.

"Well, here we are home again."

"This isn't home."

"It's where you live."

"I most certainly do not." And when I stood in the doorway of her room to leave, her eyes grew huge with tragedy. She turned her face to the window and said in an operatic voice, "Goodbye, forever!"

I gave up on taking her home. She became the Countess of Monte Cristo.

"You put me in this place, but I won't stay here. They know about you." She was my prisoner, a victim of family politics, and Evening Dale was a fake nursing home, authentic only in its odors and its nightstands. She was my sly captive, waiting for the right moment to escape.

I had my own doubts about the home—the corn soup, the butterscotch pudding, and the undertrained aides who made their rounds grudgingly. I saw it as a case study of me, proving that Americans should care for their elderly at home. What legitimized Evening Dale for me was the visiting Sunday choir whose great weight of badly sung original sin sank me into overcast, drizzling weather. This was the sound and the feel of a real nursing home.

> On a hill far away, stood an old rugged cross,
> The emblem of suffering and shame;
> And I love that old cross where the dearest and best
> For a world of lost sinners was slain.

The choir of the Calvary Evangelical Free Mission of God's Holy Word was doctrinally opposed to harmony and synchronicity. They sang hymns the way movie crowd extras said, "Rhubarb, rhubarb." The faith that bound them together transcended tempo, key, and music lessons. They stood mingled like primitive Christians with their backs to a catacomb wall, while a lion stalked the halls of the nursing home.

I would never again walk my mother down to the activities room for these song fests. I tried to explain to the nursing home's social director. "I just think the effect of the singing is more poignant at a distance, especially when you can't see them. Like the background music in a movie. Mother and I are sitting here in our one-hundred-and-thirty years of teeming consciousness, our cunning and wit pitted against the most terrible forces that Satan can put into the field. But— we are backed by the Sweet Singers of Original Sin."

"What in the world are you talking about?"

I had thought she was asleep, but she looked vigilant, suspicious, pursing her lips and glaring.

"I'm answering Tracy's question, Mother."

She looked to the social director for help with her bad boy. "He always has an answer. And he has an answering machine. He's never home when I call him. I was amazed by how lucid she could be at times. She was, of course, right.

"I wish you'd take that dreadful thing to the dump."

"I know I'm not home very much, but how will I know that you've called when I'm not home? It helps me keep in touch with you. It helps me keep track of your five calls a day."

"I don't call you five times a day."

"Okay. Not every day, but yesterday," and I held up five fingers. "But I'm sure you don't remember."

"Oh, just shut up!" This was as bad as the arguing ever got. She would lose the thread of the argument. I would feel ashamed. At least she couldn't remember what we said anymore. When I was fifteen, we had had arguments that were mostly her quotations from previous arguments. Nothing was ever erased. Now the erase mode was on nearly all the time.

"I read in the *Tribune* about some incident up at Grand Valley State. Somebody burned a cross on campus. Some KKK-style thing. Didn't you tell me that campus was built on land that was your uncle's farm around the turn of the century?"

Where?"

"Grand Valley State, between Holland and Muskegon. Wasn't that your Uncle Martin's farm when you were a child?"

"What happened to the farm?"

"It became a campus. But you used to say how your family would drive out into the country on a Sunday to visit the farm."

"Oh, yes. Uncle Martin was my favorite uncle. He was such a nice man. We would drive out after church."

"Was that when the car stalled, and your dad left you all sitting in the middle of a country road?" Priming her stories, I was at my best so long as I didn't interrupt them. While she talked, I would tell myself the story.

"I do not like a car," her father said in his stubborn staccato. "I will not drive a car." So, at fifteen, Ruth learned to drive the Ford, for which her father would pay a humbling price on a Sunday drive in the hot July dust of the country road from Uncle Martin's farm. With three daughters bunched in the back seat, Mom beside him, and the car stalled two miles from town, Dad stared down the road. They watched him step down from the car and walk wordless toward town. When he at last disappeared behind a low rise, Mom said, "Start the car, Ruth." Which she did, with a few cranks. In the back seat, her sisters grinned sideways.

"Now drive us home without any more stops." Mom was formulating the punishment, and as the car approached Dad after half-a-mile, she said over the clatter of the motor, "Don't stop." And added, even louder, "Don't slow down and don't look back." So they all stared straight ahead and didn't see Dad's face where he stood, the dust from the tires swirling and settling on his black suit. Later, when he walked into the house, he took from the shelf a volume of Spinoza and sat for an hour in apparent philosophical transfixion. Ruth peeked around the corner into the parlor and saw that he was not wearing his reading glasses.

Sometimes I showed a short movie in my head in which mother was a teenage heroine of the silent screen, one of the first women drivers in history, leaping to safety with Buster Keaton just before the train demolished the car she was driving.

At lunch in the nursing home's dining room one day, she slapped at the hand of a thin man in a long, drool-stained shirt when he leaned across the table and reached for the chocolate cake on the tray of a woman eating macaroni with her knife. Across the room an aide called out, "Dallas, sit down!" and Mrs. Connolly looked up from the soup in which she had placed her wedding rings to ask, amazed, "Alice is in town?"

I admired Mrs. Connolly's lack of inhibition, a perk of senility. She was the Comeback Queen of Evening Dale. Once when she had poked listlessly at her sandwich with a fork, I, sitting at my mother's elbow, said, "You can pick your sandwich up, you know," to which Mrs. Connolly replied in a kindly voice, "And you can shove it up your ass." I saw this freedom as a privilege of age, in the fashion of old men who salvaged the loud, plaid, polyester pants of their youth and wore them to the grocery store as if they were football alumni or golfers. When I turned seventy, the world would forgive me everything.

In the meantime, I was living out her life. On another day, after some other lunch, as I later built the story out of pieces I was told, my mother walked with her walker back down the corridor of numbered doors, guessed wrong, turned in at Room 108, paused in the doorway to look around a room she had never been in before, decided the bed by the window was hers, and sighed gratefully. When she reached the bedside, she found a tissue in her smock and wiped her watering eyes.

Her height had telescoped to less than five feet so she could not easily get into bed without a footstool, which was back in her own room. She felt that something was missing. Laying herself face-down across the too-high bed, she began to crawl up onto it, like an exhausted swimmer crawling ashore. She rested, breathing hard, before she rolled to her side, turned herself to the bed's length, laid on her back, and stared at the ceiling for several minutes before she closed her eyes.

From the doorway, his mouth sagging at one corner in an expressionless drool, Dallas Fowler had watched her get into bed, and then he shuffled to a bewildering rendezvous with her. This day he had already marathoned through the halls of the nursing home. Not once in all the miles had either foot left the tile floor, and at his pace he wandered into every room—into the activities room, the dining room, the kitchen, the nursing station, into restrooms and closets, and each time he was chased out—from in front of the loud television, from a table where a cook was stirring pudding, from the medicine cart where an aide had spilled laxative, from a restroom where a visitor was pulling up her pantyhose, from a laundry closet acrid with detergent. Sometimes he stood for several minutes in front of a door he could not open, his head down, like a dog waiting to be let in.

In his own room at the side of his own bed, he looked at my mother and thought he would like to lie down. He could not see that there was no room for him. He didn't try to push her out of bed or to lie against her or on her. Slippers falling from his feet, he simply tried to get into a bed that already had someone in it. What once might have been a physics problem of space and matter for Dallas Miller was no longer a problem.

But for my mother, the drooling face above her was a problem. She pushed him away from her and off the bed, where he staggered and stared out of a blank face. She sat up, and when Dallas again moved toward the bed, she put up her fists like Jim Jeffries in the first round on the Fourth of July in 1910.

"I'll sock you in the nose," she said, but Dallas didn't budge. At this moment a nurse passed the doorway with a medicine cart, stopped and waved to an aide to come and watch.

"The clash of the munchkins." But when nothing happened, the nurse stepped between them like a referee and escorted my mother back to her room.

"What did you think you were going to do back there?" the nurse asked.

"Back where?"

"After that boxing match, I'll bet you're ready for a nap." The nurse helped her onto her stool and into bed, taking her glasses off for her and laying them on the nightstand. Fifteen minutes later, when I arrived, she was sleeping, so I slid soundlessly into the easy chair in the corner of the room. The humming of a vacuum cleaner down the corridor was the last thing I heard as I fell asleep in the flowered chair of my childhood, and in my sleep I lifted my feet dumbly as I read, while my mother vacuumed around me.

Behind the nursing home, a waste removal truck had paused before emptying a stuffed dumpster. Neither the surge of shifting weight nor the truck's leviathan slide down the sloping service drive and into Room 104 of the Evening Dale Nursing Home got the napping driver's attention, but fracturing siding and wall studs and shattering glass and plaster woke him up into his truck from where he could see the startled eyes of my mother, who was sitting on the side of the bed two feet in front of his bumper. I jumped out of sleep, holding out both hands as if I could stop the already-stopped truck.

"You can't park here," my mother crowed in the voice of a weary teacher, and with her plastic back-scratcher she banged three times on the hood of the truck as if she were calling the room to order. But the chunk of drywall that had fallen into her lap became a piece of stone in the foundation of the house on 9th Street, and by the time the nurses and the aides and the dieticians began to crowd into her room, she was dabbing with a tissue at the blood that trickled from a cut on the back of her hand and reciting the Twenty-third Psalm: "He leadeth me beside the still waters. Lo, though I walk through the valley. . . ."

"Are you all right, Ruth? Let's take care of this little nick," an aide said, as I scooped my mother up off the bed and carried her like a small child out of the room. Vernon Ailmer from Room 106 was standing in the doorway.

"Goodbye, Sue," he mourned, reaching out to pat her, but she swatted his hand with the back-scratcher. "Sioux City Sue."

He doesn't know who I am," she grumped.

"It's okay, Mother. He's your neighbor. You're his Sioux City Sue." And I sang a few bars while she stared at my mouth.

> Sioux City Sue, Sioux City Sue,
> Your eyes are red, your hair is blue,
> I'd swap my horse and dog for you—

But now that she was on her way to the nursing station for first aid, she may have been in the driveway on 9th Street, watching Dad as he scowled at the chipped stones on the corner of the house where he had just crashed the two-day-old 1920 Ford. Inside the stunned house and facing the end of human history, her mother was on her knees, praying for paradise.

After setting her down in the nursing station to be patched up, I went back to her room to inspect the damage, remembering how

Evening Dale had seemed a safe, maximum-security nursing home when I'd settled her here. I'd read about residents wandering away from nursing homes, but I hadn't thought of trouble from the outside in. I carried her walker back to the nursing station.

"Would you like to ride up into Michigan with me for the afternoon?"

"We are in Michigan."

"We're in Indiana. Back home in Indiana."

"Indiana is not my home."

"Well, it is and it isn't." I hadn't yet grown habitual in validating her version of her life. I had the concept, but I didn't like it. Going along with wrong-headedness had seemed wrong to me. She was staring at me accusingly. She sometimes wrapped me up in riddle talk.

"Did you ever remarry?"

"Sure, I got married again."

"Whom did you marry this time?"

"Well, right now I'm not married."

"You just said that you married again."

"That's right, Mother." I didn't try to explain that I was divorced again, that I lived alone. I didn't like to think of myself being alone. Like the unemployed who said they were between jobs, I sometimes said that I was between wives. "I have a dog."

"I certainly hope you don't keep it in the house."

"Yeah, Mother, I do. She sleeps with me." Blueberry didn't.

"Animals should live outside, Stuart."

"That's what my ex-wife said."

"Don't you think you ought to have divorced me first?"

"Who do you think I am?"

"I know perfectly well who you are."

"So who do you think I am?"

"Stuart."

"You think I'm your ex-husband."

"I think nothing of the kind. I don't have an ex-husband."

"Look at me, Mom. I'm your son."

"Don't you think I know that?

"Good, Mother, that's good. Why don't we take a walk around the courtyard?"

"Did you leave the children alone?"

"What?"

"Is someone watching the children?"

"I'm your son, not your husband, and considering how much you disliked him—"

"Why, I never disliked Stuart!"

"You divorced him, didn't you?"

"I most certainly did not!"

I hated myself for arguing the unarguable. "We can drive into Berrien County." I imagined the vineyards north of Berrien Springs, green and winding among the hills.

"Where is that?"

"In Michigan."

Heading north in the car, I felt tired and old. I wasn't sure when I first began to think so continually of my age and my mortality. In a public talk when I was 37, I said that, according to the actuarial tables, I had half my life left to live and that was a lot of time. But the old math no longer worked. Now that my mother was 84, I didn't calculate the fraction of life left to me. My doctor told me cheerfully that, if I lived to the end of the century, given the progress of medical technology and family genetics, I would probably live to be 100, but I could only think how little useable time remained. When the car crossed the state line, I announced that we were entering Michigan.

"I can tell," she said.

"What gave it away?"

"I can just tell. It feels different."

"You don't miss much, do you, Mother?" That she did miss very much was often my good fortune. On trips to the doctors—for the pain in her spine or for the Richardson screw that had worked loose and now protruded from her femur, pushing against her translucent skin, and on trips to the dentist for a survey of the ruins of her mouth—we had stopped at lights behind pickup trucks with crude bumper stickers.

From a bumper cartoon of male genitals on legs chasing female genitals on legs, she had read aloud, "JUST ONE THING AFTER ANOTHER. What is that supposed to mean?"

"I don't know, Mother. I don't get it. Didn't Henry Ford say that?" Beyond the vineyards, I kept driving without any plan till we were nearly an hour north of Evening Dale.

She was biting her lip again. "We'd better be getting back home. We shouldn't leave the children alone for very long."

"The kids are fine. They're old enough to look after themselves."

"Mary's still a tyke. We'd better be getting back home."

"Mary's fine." I patted her hand. "I'm right here, Mom."

"I need to use a bathroom."

"Right away?"

"I'm afraid I'm going to have an accident."

"Just one thing after another, right? Just one accident after another."

Three months later she was gone, and I was in Michigan again on the same highway, on a last country ride home to Holland, her ashes sitting beside me. I had not been sure how to travel with her. She was my mother, and my mother rode in the passenger seat. I had first put the mahogany obelisk in the front seat, but when I started to fasten the seat belt around it, I felt ridiculous, stood up abruptly, and hit my head. If this were a hearse, I thought, she would be honored cargo. So I put her in the trunk, saying, "Think of this as your half-way house, Mother."

The strip malls and added stoplights of Holland confused me, and I nearly turned the wrong way onto 9th Street, but then I found my way to Kollen Park, where the grassy slopes still looked the same. I drove slowly down to the shore of old Black Lake. The late October sun felt warm when I parked, but when I got out of the car, my eyes began to water in the sharp wind off the choppy water.

I lifted the obelisk from the trunk and carried it under one arm to the water's edge. A story here in the deep water was nearly as old as my mother. A drowned, blue-faced child was lifted from the lake, and my mother's fear of water grew—for herself, for her children, and for their children.

I turned and walked up through the park to the entrance and along the road to 9th Street, and there was the great stone house of her childhood, with its windowed turret swelling from one corner of the third floor. I imagined the high, black, angular Ford, stuttering up the driveway and lurching against the house, and I inspected the stone corner where my grandfather had made his declaration: "I will not drive a car."

"There's nothing here, not a chip. Not a scratch." And I imagined that the wind and the rain across the eon of her life had worn the collision away. Climbing the front steps to the long porch, I saw for the first time that the white pillars were gone. The old porch roof was propped on thin black posts. No one answered my knocking, so I sat at the top of the steps and set her ashes on the porch beside me.

The front door opened, and a man called to me. "You want something?" Then, "What's your deal, man? You lost?"

"No, my mother used to live here." I was staring out across the cold lake. I turned and looked at the man's socks. "How long have you lived here?"

"Last year. A while. Look, what do you want?"

"This is my mother's home."

"This is not a home, man. This is apartments."

"Apartments?"

"Yeah, apartments. See the mailboxes?" I looked at the mailboxes and turned back toward the lake.

The man came out, the door banging closed behind him. "You got problems? You want me to call somebody?"

"Do you mind if we just sit here?"

"Maybe I better call somebody."

"We won't stay long, okay? I used to sit here on these steps in the summer. My mother used to swing on the porch swing. And my grandmother. She rubbed citronella on my back. Mosquitoes."

"What's the wood thing you got there?" The man's socks came part way down the steps.

"This? Oh, it's an urn. My mother's ashes." I patted the obelisk. "It looks sort of like a metronome."

"Jesus, man, you're carrying your mom around in a box?" The socks returned up the steps.

I looked at the mailboxes again. "It's hard to believe the old house got cut up into apartments."

"Buddy, time for you to go. You and your mom."

"We leave the house in your hands, friend. My Grandpa George's blacksmith shop was just down 8th street. Back about 1943, he built an iron grape arbor in the backyard. Painted green. Still there?"

"Grape arbor? There aren't no grapes." We headed back to the car.

"Dropping in like this wasn't such a good idea, Mother. Can't say I blame the guy." Across the street the sugar beet factory and the railroad tracks with the cars piled high with beets were all gone—as though they never were.

An hour later on the gravel shoulder of the Red Arrow Highway, we parked beside long fences of picked and leafless vines. My mother's urn sat belted in the passenger seat. She was still in Michigan. Above the vineyard, the red and yellow balloon no longer breathed a dry, sore, fevered sound. I heard a tired hurrah exhale on a distant western wind.

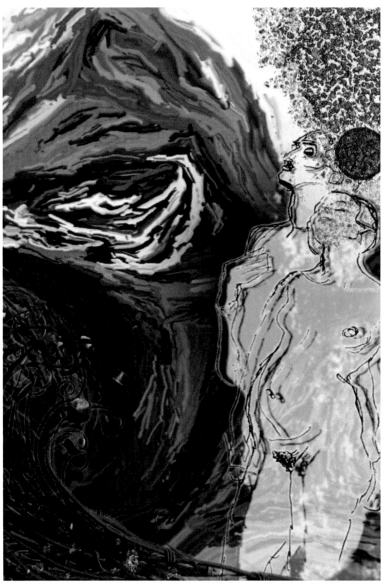

Cyndi Vander Ven

DETUMESCENCE

It's not just cowards who die many deaths. Most of us die serially, dropping away, sometimes in silence, like published poems, sometimes clattering like pots and pans. Slowly across the decades, the frog in each of us comes to a boil. Even though we catch glimpses of our decline in mirrors and store window reflections, the art of denial gets flexed and honed for the twilight of our days, when some of us will refuse to surrender our car keys.

Since a lot of the elements of decline are readily available on the periodic table, I'll sing the "Ballad of Detumescence" as my contribution to the list of greatest hits. My earliest memory of infantile erections is of a little boy stepping out of the bathtub. I wasn't even aware that I was fondling myself until my mother swatted my hand and said something like "Ahkey!" Whether that has Dutch origins or is a universal sound of disgust out of human prehistory, I knew what it meant by the tone and the expression on her face. Don't touch yourself! Don't even act like you have a penis unless you have to pee, and then aim straight!

I don't remember much of the later stages of arousal until I was around twelve when all the talk among the neighborhood boys was about the discovery of jerking off and coming. It was years before the words, "masturbate" and "orgasm," made my vocabulary list. Sex education was all slang, neighborhood lore, guesswork, and misinformation. If there was pornography around, the source was very remote and inaccessible to me until I was about sixteen. Sometime around the fifth grade, our cousin Jim from faraway Iowa visited us in Michigan. He was a little older than my two brothers in high school, and I was both enthralled and bewildered by the stories he told us of driving with friends across the state line into Omaha to spend an evening on a college campus, smelling girls' bicycle seats. He didn't describe the aroma, and his motivation, to me, was only vaguely sexual, but his hushed, knowing tone of secrecy carried an indisputable truth. This guy had information about women that was news to me.

At thirteen, when orgasm itself actually arrived during some fierce masturbation, I was shocked. I had not been warned. I might as well have stuck my penis into a light socket. Sure that I had done myself a great injury, I collapsed, torn with the usual thoughts of what my mother would say when I had to go to the hospital. AHKEY! AHKEY! But I lost no time in trying it again. It was more exciting than reading John Steinbeck, Thomas Hardy, or Victor Hugo. Naturally, despite the dangerously high voltage, I couldn't wait to do it again.

Years later she despaired of my prurience, by then compounded with heresies and enriched with exclamations such as "Geez." Recalling fondly my pre-pubescent childhood, she said, "And you were always such a good little boy!" (She could herself when really angry clench her little fists and shudderingly say, "Hell's bells!")

Skipping the middle years of sexual discovery and missteps, since this book is about the end years, I'm going to dwell now on the ebb of testosterone, as well as the therapies for prostate cancer. Age, surgery, radiation, and hormone therapy are four of the three furies warring against the libido, so powerful a vampiric creature, so ravenously passionate, that we drape it in cultural narratives of romance, monogamy, and theology. We want to legitimize but not belittle the pleasure.

Not till I waved a tired goodbye to my libido did I realize how much it had fueled my life. And I don't believe I was, even in the driven, luxurious years, exceptionally sexual. After I recovered from my mother, although I may have become less socially constrained and inhibited than some men, I was just another gland dispensing testosterone and massaging the prostatic nerves.

Everyone knows that testosterone production declines with age, though even in the post-erectile stage the male gaze continues its habitual radar scan of the female anatomy. Hips at eleven o'clock. Thighs at two-thirty. All of which becomes a prelude to nothing.

So know this, know ye this! Men don't know anything about the libido's power till they've reached the point in their prostate cancer therapy that they need to have injections of Lupron or Firmagon. Or, maybe castration, when the ornaments themselves come down from the tree. Only then do we get it.

I haven't forgotten about sexual desire. I just don't feel it except as a memory. To the point that I sometimes wonder why it was such a big deal. It was a big deal; I know that. Roosters and drakes really enjoy their violent work. Watching love scenes in movies, it's clear that lovers are having a great time, but I also want to say to them, "Hey, wear yourselves out. Soon enough you'll be looking forward to bed as the hammock of your iPad, the *New York Times* news, and e-books into the early morning hours."

The Trouble with Sleep

From the files of the Department of Unusable Foreknowledge:
"[The holy shepherd Cuthbert] . . . found that it was one of the shepherds, a worthy man, who, having incautiously mounted a tree, had fallen down, and died from the bruise, at the same time that the man of God [Cuthbert] had seen the vision." (Venerable Bede writing here.) "It was then plain to all that the holy man possessed in his mind an abundant spirit of prophecy; for that he saw before his eyes at the moment the man's soul carried to heaven, and knew beforehand what was afterwards going to be told him by others."

New Revised Standard Version of Bede:
1. A shepherd falls from a tree and dies.
2. Cuthbert at that moment in another location has a vision of the man's soul carried to heaven.
3. Others will tell him what he already knows.
4. His vision confirms the faith of believers in an afterlife of reward or suffering.

Such transcendent vision, concurrent with events, has no practical, event-altering application, though it might be a guide to those still waivering between darkness and faith. But it must have become annoying for Cuthbert always saying to people, "Yes, I already know." The closest I've come to that is seeing on Atlanta TV a field goal scored six seconds before a viewer sees it in Ohio. Not enough time to place a bet.

But the Cuthbert story is a fine and bracing tale to tell the next generation to die: in the shadow of the mystery of life, sleeping and dying shall be like the mounting and falling from a tree, and the dying and the carrying up to heaven shall be seen by another as in a vision. A mystery, more or less, almost a DNA-style helical rising and falling, both in sleeping and dying, when all we really want to do is to nap without interruption.

Even before the burden of prophecy, the trouble begins with sleep, the circadian letting go when the body and mind say enough is enough for a while, but when synchronicity isn't always in play, as when the body sits propped in a meeting of suits, and the poor, bored mind drops its jaw and a string of J's skitters across the laptop's keyboard. As when the body, exhausted with chain-sawing a storm-struck tree, goes down itself like a tree, but the anxiety over a failing marriage hangs by shoelaces from the electrical wires swarming inside the skull, the eyes staring up at the domed ceiling.

Not all the trouble is indoors. As recently as 1250 BCE, Odysseus, the swineherd's best friend, had to sleep some of the time and in strange places. Google "Odysseus sleep" and you get countless sites that want to talk about whom he slept with. For the quiz, it was Circe and Calypso. For extra credit, mention "epic euphemism," the first known reference to sex as sleeping. Homeric scholars continue to debate whether two lovers in twenty years constituted "sleeping around" (BCE rules apply).

But one time Odysseus just prayed for guidance and fell asleep alone, and then his men killed and ate the cattle of the god Helios, which was both a defiance of their leader's orders and a sin against the gods. When most of us wake up, not having men at our command, and not dreaming prophetic visions, we suffer only the neurotic sense of having sinned against ourselves—squandered our own lives' precious time in sleep.

Then the tide of day seizes us, and we are swept away, immersed in errands, waiting rooms (death-in life experience), gossip, and bodily functions. If we wholly enter into the day's moment, "dilate our ego," so that the evanescent moment is inseparable from perpetual being, don't we simultaneously depart the moment? Unless dilation delivers us through the ego's birth canal into the presence of both life and death, we haven't really seized the day in all its meaning, have we? Every day is a day in the life of dying. Shouldn't we KNOW that in the fullness of our awareness? Or is that a state of being beyond knowing?

If we don't gaze fully and lovingly on the misting sea and its hazed horizon and stare into the maw of the monstrous, globe-shrouding surf that can kill us without even noticing us, then we are still on the inside looking in at ourselves. Exhibit: a girl of fourteen sits in Costa Rica on the edge of the ocean, softly merging with the sand beneath her and the froth of water around her legs and, shading her eyes to see new messages on her cell phone, surrenders herself to the great earth's water cycle as she pees into the Pacific.

Though humans have not always been so institutionalized and technologized, we have always multitasked, used social networks, and paced like Sophocles did beside his Aegean Sea, or sat like the Tica beside the Pacific, designing narratives out of starry constellations or text messages. It's what the brain has always been doing at the water's edge; it's what happens when a Victorian poet imagines the surf curling and crashing around the head of a Greek playwright while revising a script 2,500 years ago or when a fourteen-year-old brain meets a four-billion-year-old ocean while texting and sexting with a guy she thinks is sixteen, but who is actually forty-seven.

We live in layers of time and by indirection, and we talk about our lives in the swirl of the order and disorder of language. Years ago in the English corridor at Indiana University South Bend, there was an office door bearing the legend that the great thing about language is that it never sticks to the subject at hand. Which is to say that language articulates a kind of healthy, exploratory Attention Deficit Disorder, never more evident than when we think about death and when we deny it. And when we have elastic fantasies of sex, which are mostly about power, surrender, and stage business: Dim lighting. Seducer enters. Lingerie goes flying. What was I saying? Oh, we deny and we die. And sleep is the warm-up act.

In *Dragons of Eden*, Carl Sagan writes that we sleep in layers of time, our bodies reluctant to let go of balance and control, flinching with the primordial fear of falling from trees. No wonder we need lullabies and stories to prop us securely on branches. And there are those adults who claim a few dormant hours every night with a television screen flickering its senseless light around the cave. As a child, my son wrote a poem in which he felt in his bed at night that "darkness caved in the door." That's when a house and family are meager defense against boundless, sightless oblivion. When in my Costa Rican mountain night,

> The magician tree turns black
> against the fading glass and flattens
> to a curtain of the nocturnal mind,
> teatro oscuro.

These lines are themselves another curtain pulled across the oblivion that looms over consciousness. A rhythmic defacing, like a graffito signed on a corner of night. We can't entirely face or efface death, but we're pretty adept at decorating sleep.

2. The Holy Unknowable

Although I'm playing a delaying game with an inexorable but non-aggressive cancer, I feel a great peacefulness with my lovely, loving wife. We've reached a place of serene, sometimes silly, love and paldom. Having been passionate lovers, we're now devout companions, living as honestly as we can in the face of the body and mind's eventual failure and death.

Because Cyndi is many years younger than I, the probability is great that I will die before her. That she will live on, perhaps for many years, is not made bearable by remembering human history. Countless lovers have watched each other die and found ways to endure, but the sorrow does not diminish. Loss is loss and cannot be denied. Cyndi, believing deeply in an afterlife of salvation, wishes for my conversion

so that I, too, will share in a bountiful eternity. Raised in Congrega-
tional and Methodist churches, I fell from faith as a teenager and never
returned. I live in the cheerful unknowing of agnosticism, not defiant
of the possibility of a personal god, but not able to comprehend one or
even wish for one. If I could believe for her, I would.

We two find so much comfort and reward in simply being together,
holding each other, or watching some subtitled psychological drama
or an inane action movie of hallucinogenic special effects. We read
to each other at night from *The English Patient, Extremely Loud and
Incredibly Close, The Street of Crocodiles,* and *Eating Animals.* We prepare
meals in our minority vegetarian world, surrounded by the criminal
tsunami of factory farming, stumbling once in a while into seafood and
even falling weakly for a Zaxby's chicken sandwich. Nurturing two live
puppies and two stuffed monkeys gives us a version of family that will
endure till we have to surrender—we hope many years from now, so
long as pain and fog don't overcome us.

Cyndi has been a caring influence for me over the past nineteen
years. Living with her and aging together have given me a greater
capacity for empathy and the forgiveness it enables. I feel less con-
frontational, less judgmental, less vulnerable, and more able to walk
for a time in the heavy boots of others. She has a generosity that I love
so much and that I try to make a part of my way of living. She senses
when we can help someone, while I'm more likely to see someone's
need fatalistically. More than a decade ago, we learned indirectly of
an administrative decision at Indiana University South Bend that was
about to gravely affect the career of our good friend, then Vice Chan-
cellor of Academic Affairs, Les Lamon. A first-rate teacher, scholar,
community servant, and administrator, whose presence and leadership
at IUSB made it a so much better institution, his service had come into
conflict with the institutionally destabilizing policies and decisions of
Chancellor Ken Perrin. I grieved for what was about to happen. Cyndi
simply said, "You have to tell him," which I did. Les acted preemptively
and went on till retirement to teach history and serve as Director of
the Civil Rights Heritage Center, which he had worked to create as an
archive and forum for the history of civil rights in Northern Indiana.

Learning to walk together less shadowed by blaming and being blamed for the errors and wrongs of a lifetime, Cyndi and I still have to shrug off those shadows from time to time. A comforting friend once said to me, "Don't think of an ended marriage as a failure. We learn and grow from loss." Another said: "Other people on this faculty have had lots of relationships that ended. The only difference is that you married all of your girlfriends." Well, not quite. Not *all*. But an indecent number! And with so much stress and disappointment inflicted on more or less innocent bystanders. The unsweepable debris of divorce. Then untangling the heaped and knotted kelp of intimate storms for one more try at love and companionship.

Where do we find the hope and the will to begin? And then begin again? The untiring surge against the Dover strand. When finally the tide subsides, as it has, and we lovingly and gratefully hold each other's hand along a beach in St. Augustine or on the jetty in Howth, or softly into sleep above the night-quiet Hauptbahnhof in Innsbruck, or among our unknowable neighbors in a suburb of Atlanta, how has the peace come to us? Rather than bone-deep fatigue and aging brains, is it an authentic wisdom of years of discovery? However it is, we have it, and, oh, how we need it as age bears us off like blind pilgrims into the traveled, pathless forest!

Learning to let go, particularly of guilt and blaming, is the best mental health, at breakfast, lunch and dinner, and in the act of falling asleep and waking up, when sensory deprivation raises a curtain on *the past*. Learning's an act of forgiving, both forgiving oneself and others. Digging our nails into the already gouged past exhausts a field with the same unrotated crop on the Farm of Victims and Survivors. Somewhere Saul Bellow wrote about our living in a culture in which seventy-year-olds still can't forgive their parents for toilet-training them. A student of mine once wrote of the psycho-bludgeoning of her siblings in an abusive family: "And some of us nearly survived." Another said she had been scarred by that horrific moment when her father was about to kick a chair out from under her mother to hang her from a rope in the garage. He let her mother down when she told him she was about to wet herself.

"Immedicable woes" of humanity's toiling, oppressed generations abound, a la Edwin Markham and Jean-François Millet. And maybe the woes of the son angrily disappointed by his father, and the daughter offended and unforgiving of her mother are no less and no less escapable. How do we throw off such loss before we die?

How do we come to the moment when we can feel—not just say, but feel—that enough is enough and no more? If we can't, then we're writing a narrative of victimhood in which our significance lies in the suffering inflicted upon us. We suffer irreparably, but there—there—lies the cause. Stage direction: *light fades as slumped figure points off into shadows.*

The spirit of victimhood makes us poor subjects of the cosmos—which maybe we are? Cassius to Brutus: "The trouble lies not in our stars," Cassius says to Brutus, "… but in ourselves that we are underlings." I say all this out of an entire life growing up and old in the fortunate American middle-class of the mid- and latter twentieth century, with educated parents, good schools, good health, and a growing economy. I felt, too, an intermittent confidence that progressivism was not merely dreamy hope but an emerging world of equality for women and minorities. Both historically and planetarily, it was a small bubble of comfort. I didn't grow up in a rusting favela in Rio or on hardscrabble Akill Island. What do I know about immedicable woe? *Nada y pues nada. Nada mas.*

At seventy-four, I drink a cup of decaf coffee in the morning, green tea the rest of the day, write, read online news, walk the dog, get lost among the rabbit warrens of the Internet, cook, follow the Braves in their pursuit of the currently unstoppable Nationals, and have talks, great and small, with Cyndi, and via Internet with family, friends, and former students. While it all appears very ordinary and predictable, we are still surprised by living, looking up from a field or away into a stand of trees as if to ask, "Who's there?" Numinous moments rise before us like stars and grasshoppers, if not divine, then holy, in the way that I've been discussing it with my friend of many years, Chuck Stewart, himself living an enhanced exile as an expatriate in Nova Scotia. We discussed our exile from the Other that is the

Cosmos in the summer of 2012, focusing on Jared Carter's poem, "Up in Michigan":

CS. *What most intrigues me is the notion of the "holy" or the "sacred" in this poem. Many years ago I read Rudolf Otto's "The Idea of the Holy." Otto tries to describe the phenomenology of the holy, the sacred, the ineffable – what he calls an "Überschuss" — "something more." It's an experience that defies rational categorization. Otto labeled it the experience of the "numinous" that is present in all religions, both theistic and non-theistic. This is not "holy" as something with moral value; this is the sense of "something other," which Otto said was "nicht Begriffene und Verstandene," which means something that cannot be conceptualized and intellectualized.*

TV. Cyndi urged me to read theology several years ago when she was in the MTS program at Candler School of Theology at Emory, but I was not an eager or very willing student, particularly of abstract, theoretical theology. The idea of the holy does interest me very much, but picture me on a ladder at the side of a cathedral in Rome, trying to peer through the stained glass darkly, or walking among the ruins of the sixth century Irish monastery, Clonmacnoise, pausing to absorb the impenetrable immensity of time and space as it surrounds the ruins of "a serious house on serious ground." Exile's state of aloneness eases some in knowing there are others, such as my friend and pastor, James Lamkin, who has in him a deep sense of the exiled consciousness, pastoring as he does to the bruised and broken among his congregation.

For me the ultimate reality of the divine remains a paradox, in that, despite Dickinson's assertion that the "brain is wider than the sky," human consciousness seems to have opened a great and mysterious space between our self-awareness and our cosmic-awareness as our fingertips touch starlight. So, does our sense of the numinous constitute a connection between our neurons and heart muscles and some immeasurable and undefinable other presence that is the all of being? Or do we project our sense of our own Dickinsonian "wideness" onto the material cosmos, which may or may not be a kind of supersentience?

After writing the word, *supersentience,* I wondered if there were such a word afoot in the world. Turns out there is, and it seems to be a state of knowing that is beyond knowing, a not-knowing, which takes us back to the idea of an ineffable holiness. Can we agree that the feeling or sensation is itself, on some level, real? It's origin? It's meaning? Can we distinguish between the holy and the divine?

CS. *The experience of the holy, of the numinous, is connected with what Otto calls the "mysterium tremendum," which is that ultimate perhaps unknowable reality of the divine, to recall the Wakefield quote at the top of the poem ("How do we know when it's God?"). The experience of the numinous brings with it that sense of terror and awe that the Romantics frequently wrote about when they spoke of the sublime. Think of Wordsworth in "The Prelude" when he describes rowing toward a mountain in the Lake District and feeling a sense of dread, awe, and wonder (more awe and wonder than dread, however) as the mountain loomed increasingly overhead. It's that sense of the "wholly other" that brings with it what the main character of Carter's poem experiences—a sense of existential dread.*

TV. I have felt such existential dread many times in my life, most notably on the shore of any ocean, a few times at the edge of a vast and darkening forest, and on the summit of one of the mountains in the Alps high above Innsbruck in 2009. Dread is the word, and it is born for me of the realization that my consciousness stands (cowers?) in exile before the vastness that surrounds me so indifferently, a vastness enhanced by modern science's estimates of the cosmos as having between 100 and 300 sextillion stars. But, hey, who's counting when we're filled with dread?

CS. *Otto expanded his notion of the mysterium tremendum to include "fascination," also an element, perhaps, of the main character's experience in Carter's poem:*

> A light switched on. When his pupils
> adjusted, he could look all the way up
> both barrels, as though peering into
> two long, metallic tunnels, and see
> far away, like stars, the paper wadding
> of each shell, bunched up, crimped,
> ready to enter his brain.

With what could be the instrument of his death, the narrator has a strange sense of fascination, an attention to detail, as he gazes up through those "metallic tunnels" to peer at "far away, like stars, the paper wadding/ of each shell, bunched up/crimped/ready to enter his brain." The "far away/ like stars" bring in an element of almost unknowable cosmic distance, those black, vast reaches of space that underscore our existential predicament.

TV. I don't think I've read that stanza as well as you have. Now I see a haiku-like synthesis of the small immediacy of the gun-barrels and wadding with the immense and distant stars.

CS. *The main character recalls his dead father, his "retreat into nothingness" that left his face "supremely peaceful, as though/something he had encountered . . . had finally/revealed itself." Such situations "in extremis" provide the experience of the numinous, the "wholly other," but I agree with you that, in the end, the issue—"How do we know when it's God?"— remains essentially unresolved, unanswered. Unless, of course, we consider the last stanza to be the poet's conclusion: all is gnawed away, gone; the "flat stones skipping across the water" create momentary "widening circles" that "merge, then disappear."*

TV. For me, the dead face reveals no more than a return to the inert material made seemingly vast by the vacating of life from the face—of muscle tension, blood moving through the lips, and eyelids trembling. John Irving writes in *Catch-22* that when Snowden dies, Yossarian sees his organs and intestines spilling out of his body—the spirit gone, the body is garbage. Still, we might say that all being—the remains of assassination and stone and peat bog—are instances of ineffable holiness. As when we stood on a Monday in the high, blowing Featherbed of the Dublin Mountains, not far from a monument to Capt. Noel Lemass, IRA, murdered in 1923 a year after Irish independence and left there in that grassy expanse, amid white, bird-like flowers.

CS. *Wasn't it Henry James who famously said, as he was dying, something about "the distinguished thing"? Distinguished as something dignified . . . or distinguished as something "wholly other"? But there was nothing dignified or noble when the gas chambers were opened at Auschwitz, and the Sonderkommandos dragged out the naked bodies of men, women, children, their corpses mired in shit, piss, and blood. The god hanging on the gallows in Wiesel's Night strikes me as an oddly Christian, sacrificial deity.*

Yes, the figure on the gallows hangs amid such enormity of suffering and cruelty. I agree with those survivors who have said that they don't ask of the holocaust, "Why? It just was." The holy unknowable, both in the horrifying past and in the ordinary next day.

Living a life in trembling exile, with moments of supersentient consciousness, what are we to believe? We get glimpses, but of what? In his Nobel speech (1976) Saul Bellow speaks of glimpses into the universe in a way that suggests he has a sense of the holy.

The essence of our real condition, the complexity, the confusion, the pain of it is shown to us in glimpses, in what Proust and Tolstoy thought of as "true impressions." This essence reveals, and then conceals itself. When it goes away it leaves us again in doubt. But we never seem to lose our connection with the depths from which these glimpses come. The sense of our real powers, powers we seem to derive from the universe itself, also comes and goes.

If the sense of our real powers "derives from the universe itself," then human consciousness appears to hold a limited membership in a cosmic consciousness—open to the general public at times TBD. Or is our finite consciousness of Bellow's vast essence merely a mechanism, a medium, rather than a tributary flowing into the same body of music and water?

Maybe such glimpses are no more than momentary comforts, telling us that we are not alone. How else to use them? As a foundation for empathy, perhaps as a sign of the presence of a silent holiness that is, and Bellow then quotes Joseph Conrad, "the subtle but invincible conviction of solidarity that knits together the loneliness of innumerable hearts…which binds together all humanity - the dead to the living and the living to the unborn." I don't find in this almost unnerving exploration any ground claimed for one religion or world religions. It's about what Robert Frost describes in "For Once, Then, Something," peering down a well:

Once, when trying with chin against a well-curb,
I discerned, as I thought, beyond the picture,
Through the picture, a something white, uncertain,
Something more of the depths—and then I lost it.
Water came to rebuke the too clear water.

And that's about what I have come to in my reflections, humbly and in good spirits, though knowing that one critic of Frost called his poetry "the last sweepings of the Puritan latrine." Reverence for life and love for all others holds promise beyond ideologies and theologies.

3. A CASE FOR UNCERTAINTY

Around the turn of the century, I played an unofficial role as resident non-believer in a fundamentalist Baptist church in Sawyer, Michigan. This unsalaried position fell into my lap. All I had to do for success Woody Allen style was to show up. Cyndi had resumed her Protestant churchgoing when we moved across the state line from South Bend to Bridgman, and, because when we go we go together, I went along as her agnostic prince consort, her Manchu èfu. That is, until the Board of Deacons back-burnered her request for a discussion of her 25-page researched paper on biblical gender equality. It looked like they might get to it around the year 2525.

So we moved on, she on a fellowship to do graduate work in the Candler School of Theology at Emory University, Atlanta, and I to a post-retirement, salaried shadow role as an adjunct professor at the University of Georgia. Cyndi's friends would miss her, but events at that church made it clear that my cheerfully inscrutable presence would vaporize quickly from those pews. One day, during a session of Sunday-school-of-the-whole, someone said he was apprehensive when he was in the presence of non-believers, fearing that his faith might get subverted. He didn't turn around and point at me; in fact, he and I had never had a conversation about anything. Maybe it was my aura non grata, the sulphurous emanation of theological uncertainty that surrounded me—the rotten eggs of secular humanism.

During another Sunday school discussion led by the pastor, the nature of the quest to know god surfaced. At some point I volunteered that god's infinite presence would always hold some degree of mystery to the finite human mind. A woman in the back row replied instantly that there is no mystery—that the light of holy scripture fully reveals god. Which suggested that all I needed to do was open my eyes. Or dig the wax from my ears so that I could hear god's word (see Cotton Mather).

I was treated at church as a faith object, a project for conversion. The pastor's father gave me a book he thought would help me turn the corner toward Christian faith. It didn't do the job. Soon after, his earnest interest in me as a spiritually homeless exotic lost its fire.

Another man—a church deacon and occasional tennis-doubles opponent—met me for lunch several times at Hyerdall's, home of fresh biscuits, and tried to illuminate me in his faith. We discussed what seemed to me the questionable doctrine that, while god makes husbands the decision-making heads of households, women are different-yet-equal partners. I wanted to know, if guys have the power, how can women in their consulting role be equals. What evidence is there that men are divinely authorized leaders of women? He quoted the apostle Paul and then asked whether I'd noticed that god made men bigger and stronger than women. This guy was maybe 5'8" and weighed about 150. He was not wearing a Viking helmet. I was pretty sure that in his entire life he had never once stormed ashore to plunder a village. His tennis serve was a lollipop.

Such was my lot among fundamentalists. I readily admit that no person, including me, lives life free of inconsistency and contradiction. Gaps between word and action, as well as between word and word, abound, at times astounding in their authoritative, self-congratulatory flamboyance. "I'm a Christian first and a mean-spirited, bigoted conservative second, and don't you ever forget it," writes Ann Coulter, right-wing provocateur, claiming as she sometimes does that it's a joke. Years ago a good friend said that he could accomplish anything—with just a little extra push. So I did. Off a cliff. He was airborne for six seconds. It's a joke.

Add to inconsistency and contradiction, our deep well of ignorance, especially of the self, and we have the premise for the best of comedy and tragedy, much of it already written. Not knowing is an irrevocable ingredient of human consciousness.

What is so wrong about learning to say, "I don't know"? Ken Johnson at Colorado in the '60s said that the most useful statement he learned to make as a graduate student in English at USC was "I don't know." It's both a strategy to survive one's oral exams and a way to begin every day honestly. Part of the counter-argument is that the condition of not-knowing may be a basis for moral sloth and intellectual cowardice, which implies that genuine moral searching and intellectual study will lead to certainty. Just put in the hours earnestly. "Seek and ye shall find" (Matthew 7:7). But know also, know ye this, as psychologist George Miller put it, "We find what we're looking for." Or: we find what we want to find. The mighty power of predisposition.

The late Peter Stanlis, a Robert Frost and Edmund Burke scholar, philosophical conservative and devout Catholic, advised our mutual friend, Chancellor Les Wolfson, against an agnostic stance. Stanlis called agnosticism cowardice. But Wolfson is probably the only university chancellor in history to bravely and formally address in public the virtue of negative capability: "when a man is capable of being in uncertainties, mysteries, doubts, without any irritable reaching after fact and reason" [and institutional doctrine]. Wolfson loved great music and believed it was his best means to experience the vastitude of divinity. Though yearning at times for some satisfying religious membership, he resisted formal theologies. He didn't know, but might have guessed, that of the 73% of the faculty who were actually listening to his address at that moment, only seven of them were English faculty, of which two remembered that they had not been able fully to explain the concept of negative capability in their own doctoral oral exams fifteen years before. A survivor of the '60s, Wolfson would say that you've got a chance, as long as they don't shoot you.

Stanlis greatly admired Frost's poetic, patriarchal wisdom as a kind of model certainty, a staunch resistance to an entropic, universal flow of being downward to nothingness.

Our life runs down in sending up the clock.
The brook runs down in sending up our life.
The sun runs down in sending up the brook.
And there is something sending up the sun.
It is this backward motion toward the source,
Against the stream, that most we see ourselves in,
The tribute of the current to the source.
It is from this in nature we are from.
It is most us.

"West-Running Brook" has great beauty in its music and sends up a brave tribute to our human urge for order, but what that order is, what that "something" is that sends up the sun, remains an unspecified will. As is the glimpse of what—truth?—at the bottom of a well in "For Once then Something."

What was that whiteness?
Truth? A pebble of quartz? For once, then, something.

Robert Frost was himself the White Eminence of Somethingness, which he invoked in other poems as well.

Something there is that does not love a wall.
Choose something like a star.
Something has to be left to god.

Stanlis found in Frost a staunch certainty of Something, but George Nitchie dismissed Frost for offering merely "a momentary stay against confusion" which, he argued, Frost's vision never fully realized. He wrote that Frost represented "the last sweepings of the Puritan latrine." Still, Frost did kiss the frog, or at least he kissed a green Frog of Somethingness.

Something like this Somethingness appears in Saul Bellow's 1976 Nobel Prize Speech: "The essence of our real condition, the complexity, the confusion, the pain of it is shown to us in glimpses, in what Proust and Tolstoy thought of as 'true impressions.' This essence reveals, and then conceals itself. When it goes away it leaves us again in doubt." Intermittence. Evanescence. Like Frost's glimpse of something, a piece of quartz, at the bottom of the well under the daylight, pieces of love, courage, fear, and wonderment.

At Breadloaf and elsewhere, Frost was adept at his own grand public pronouncements on truth, wrapped comfortably in neighbor-at-the-fence digressions and off-hand anecdotes. He had a disarming farmer's aw-shucks, off-the-cuff style. Charming he was, when he wasn't petulant, but to read the transcripts now, without benefit of the ancient voice and the snow-browed visage, is at times a difficult ingestion. Teaching at Breadloaf throughout the '50s and till the year before his death in 1963, Frost's sinecure intersected with Saul Bellow in 1954, who said, "I thought when I was his age, people would let me get away with murder, too. But I'm not allowed to get away with a thing."

Do I drape this essay in the views of literary giants for any other reason than to shore up my own uncertain defense of uncertainty? Something like a traditional review of the literature at the onset of a dissertation, but sans footnotes—to place oneself in context, to enroll in the published conversation, to show that the writer has read something.

In an essay (2010), in Saul Bellow's *Enigmatic Love*, Norma Rosen recalls her summer of 1954 at Breadloaf as a student of Bellow. At her first tutorial, she sat at his feet (literally), awed in his presence, which was itself illumined by the heroes of his fiction and his recent Pulitzer Prize. "The hero's glance took in the random world and transformed it into one where light, falling on a house, a wall, a hillside, spoke of cosmic matters. Material things and events could be more than one knew, Bellow's novels told us, and his heroes all searched for that 'more.'"

Is it possible to view with reverence a cosmos in which one has not discovered either that there is a god or that there is no god? A cosmos in which one lives in the presence only of glimpses of something—something more? In which we do not hear voices either of god or angels or otherwise anthropomorphize the Himalayas, the Pacific's

Mariana Trench, the moon, the sun, or the boundless galaxies? Can we hold sacred a universe void of supra-humanoid consciousness and vast beyond our starved surmise? If we are it and it is us, swarming and spiraling in some great is-ness, some somethingness, is not an embracing acceptance enough?

WAKING UP SPACE

Find out today there is a third dimension,
that highways could be objects passing among other objects.
Or waves. First the car is in front of the bridge.
Then the car is painted over with a sign.

I may have known about space already
from practical use. If so,
I must have learned it after birth
but before memorytime.

The October tree once pushed air apart as it grew,
slapping space with its green hands.
On this day the tree foregrounds the forest.
The yellow leaves make a plane like ashes,
stretching off away from the tree,
learning another place.

The place we stand seems trivial,
but gulfs there are surrounding things, even leaves.
The years had flattened all these to a curtain
or a parade ground for the self, a page, not a book.

Try to think of space and objects like pages of a novel,
each page telling its own story, hiding other pages,
some stories on the backs of pages looking the other way.

Start with a close thing like a sign post
very near the roadside and try to see
how there is something that surrounds it
which you cannot see, but receptors tell you
is making something like a sound,

more constant that a chant or a dynamo.
Every year a tree blows bubbles
that look like leaves,
injects them with a juice.

Awash in an acceptance of a quotidian, galvanic is-ness, how are we then to give thanks? Let us give thanks for that which we know and for the alluring, terrifying mystery of that which we may never know. Then, how are we to forgive? Let us forgive our own and others' ignorance, fear, cruelty, and unforgivingness. Let us serve each other in kindness, and, while we're at it, try to save the planet from ourselves.

My good friend John Lewis, a political scientist who could as easily have become an astrophysicist or conductor of an orchestra, said once, as we scanned the evening sky for glimpses of satellites reflecting light off a drowning summer sun, that it isn't useful to talk about god if we aren't talking about a personal god: "Oh, all-being not-god, ever with us in our need, though you hear us as hurtling comets hear pleas, as stones below the plunge of cataracts————"

Mark Twain averred that a man viewing the Grand Canyon for the first time who falls to his knees in prayer and another man who exclaims, "Well, I'll be goddamned," are expressing the same wonder and amazement. Are these two tones a single, two-toned wondering reverence, a Faulknerian stunned amaze?

More than once in my life I have stood at the edge of the Pacific or on a mountain top in the Alps and felt lurking in that beauty beyond or below me a frightening power that I could not comprehend and could barely hold at bay. Even the stillness of a forest has the power.

I keep asking myself whether all this prose is anything more than an attempt to dignify cowardice and befuddlement? Many of us effect some degree of management through what Paul Veynes calls, in his book on whether the Greeks believed their myths, the "Balkanization" of the mind, neat and not-so-neat compartments of values that rub against each other, but which our brain system of denial and rationalization usually keeps from a head-on collision. Sacred texts affirm a god of vengeance and forgiveness. Religious faith in a world in which terrible acts occur in the presence of a god of good.

After the cruel murder of school children and their teachers in New Town, Connecticut, in December 2012, Rabbi Stephen Folberg was asked how it is possible to understand what happened.

"I saw a bumper sticker once that said, 'God is good. Evil is real. And God is all powerful. Pick two,'" Folberg says.

"The idea was to say, if one accepts those three propositions as true, then they're logically inconsistent. And how do you wiggle your way out of that issue?" You cannot wiggle your way out, the rabbi continues. You have to admit that we live in a world that is, by turns, beautiful and shattered.

So we are at inner peace and in touch with the suffering world to the extent that we can live Folberg's assertion that the world is, itself, "by turns, beautiful and shattered." We live on Planet Paradox; therefore, we think in paradox. As a professor at Paradox University, I tried to keep paradox alive in the classroom. Not all of my students were comfortable with the condition of continually becoming. But how can we definitively measure truth if it won't hold still? Well, you ride it like a wild horse till you fall off. And then you get back on. Paradox will not stop bucking. Somewhere midstream in my career as a professor, trailing clouds of glorious degrees and titles, I visited a class of high school seniors anxious about their college prospects. I told them that I was still trying to figure out what I wanted to be when I grew up. After class, one student stayed behind to chastise me for making such a statement. Clarity and irony can be awkward team teachers. Ironists must remember to wink.

Interactive classroom discourse was central to my methodology throughout my career, but I recall one course evaluation from a student who complained that she hadn't come to college to listen to other students' opinions. I had the Ph.D. I had the responsibility to present what is true. The professor should profess and not encourage untitled opinion.

I recall an undergraduate class in formal logic at the University of Michigan (circa 1957) in which a very young Professor Carl Cohen invited us during to discussion to solve a problem in logic. We mulled and buzzed for a while, and then I shot up my hand eagerly. (Another professor once called on me, saying, "VanderVen, I see you writhing back there.") I dictated a fairly lengthy series of logical steps, which Professor Cohen agreeably wrote on the chalk blackboard. After a moment, he told me in a sympathetic tone that my solution didn't work; then he smiled and thanked me for trying. I don't remember feeling wrong. In fact, I very much liked being engaged in the process.

That's the world of learning as it worked best for me. Professor Cohen was a practicing agnotologist before there was the word, inviting his students to swim around in the discovery of their own ignorance. I wish I had felt more deeply ignorant then, more humble, and more eager to learn.

I was baptized a Christian baby in a family of Protestants, serial Protestants, in that, as we moved from town to town around Michigan, we attended churches that in my parents' judgment offered them the most compatible theology to what they knew growing up in Holland, Michigan. The Christian Reformed Church of the Netherlands migrated with Dutch immigrants to Western Michigan, but we were Congregationalists for five years, and then Methodists. The CRC is Calvinist, but my father became a Lutheran in Utica, Michigan, and my mother continued her Methodist membership in Clawson, Michigan after my parents divorced. I don't recall ever hearing any discussion of salvation, how to get it, and whether you can keep it once you get it. Maybe in the pulpit, but not at home. I do remember a Methodist Santa handing out oranges in church on Christmas Eve around 1947. My mother was a thoughtful Christian with a social conscience; she despised racism and intolerance, watched with fascination the American Religious Townhall on television, eager to hear the views of priests, rabbis, and pastors of various Protestant denominations. In that sense, she fell away from her more narrow Christian Reformed beginnings. I don't think any of her four children knew the depths of her daily spiritual life; for example, I was long gone from home when I learned from her that she prayed in silence every day of her life. She was vocal about some matters of faith. Although she didn't attend church regularly, she saw that we did as children. I can picture a trail of Vander Ven children leaving the house on Sunday morning one at a time for the two block walk up Cass Avenue, as she made sure that we were clean, well-dressed for church, and on time. She didn't always make it herself. I don't remember that my father walked with us either. He had his own agenda.

My mother's parents divided their church memberships over some classic Protestant doctrinal issue which I'm not sure my mother ever explained. At some point in her childhood, her father moved his membership to another denomination, and that doctrinal separation lasted to the end of their lives. Out of the great stone and brick home on 9th Street in Holland, overlooking Lake Macatawa, George Hoekstra would turn one way, and Grace the other.

We had our own theological split, my mother and I, one Easter weekend. When she said we were going to church the next day, I declared, in the fashion of arrogant, ungenerous, rebellious youth, that I no longer believed in the resurrection so I would not go. She called me an "irreligious heathen." But what would it have cost me to go to church with her? An act of love and kindness beyond my capacity, I was a teenage reprobate. I was too absorbed in my own stubborn Protestantism. Monday night, Cyndi and I will go to a Christmas Eve service at our Northside Drive Baptist Church here in Atlanta, where tolerance is so expansive that it embraces even me. I will think of my mother, who taught me to sing the Boar's Head Carol as a little boy in Almont, Michigan, bearing into the dining room a white, empty platter with "garlands gay and rosemary." And of the Christmas Eve in 1998 when I rode down the mountain in Winter Park, Colorado, on the ski patrol sled, my right tibia and fibula in pieces. My pain management was the music of my childhood, which I sang over and over in Latin:

> Adeste Fideles, laeti triumphantes,
> Venite, venite in Bethlehem.
> Natum videte, Regem Angelorum;
>
> Venite adoremus,
> venite adoremus,
> venite adoremus
> Dominum!

I bear these fragments, these strange abutments, into my winter of contentment. Our species's kind and cruel community rises out of stories of humanity that affirm our poor and worthy beginnings, long before Abraham in the origin of our family out of Africa. I'll take a rain check on ancestral kingship.

Late in life, feeling more empathy for any religion that doesn't shun, abuse, or kill in the name of righteousness, I still can't wall off greater possibility; I'm an incorrigible, agnostic evolutionist. Without a visionary faith and oneness in some version of god, my perpetual skepticism abides. For me, a personal god has been an absent father and mother, which I write at risk that my agnosticism might be seen as growing out of my distrust of parents. But I'm an equal opportunity skeptic. We are all in exile—from the parents of our parents of our parents unto our unwritten beginnings. Ever since human consciousness began to form stories of its past—transforming a remembered African meadow into Eden and transforming our continental migrations into a theology of dispersal born of sin, humanity has lived in self- and self-conscious exile—a vast, planetary diaspora. And the path back lies not just in the memory of sacred texts, but in the discovery of the larger texts we are still writing.

During all the questioning and wondering in and out of religion and science, there come times to keep silent. And to listen. To the sounds of music in nature and in humanity. More than fifty years ago, my brother Jack and I sat at the family cherry table, squeezed into the tiny dinette space of my mother's little house in Michigan, where we talked about the choices we would make if we had to chose one work of music, and only one, for our desert island exile.

Jack argued for Bach's *Mass in B Minor.* I argued for Handel's Messiah. Nobody argued for Hoagy Carmichael's "Stardust," but it's on my short list of the greatest ballads. Our arguments haven't survived, though they might be hibernating along some neuronic path in our brains, but Jack was right. If we could discuss it again, Bach would get my vote, too. Just the transition from the Quoniam into the Cum Sancto Spiritu will light up the night sky over that desert island till the oceans rise.

Our brotherly debate found its peace a few weeks ago, when on 13 December 2012, the Atlanta Symphony Orchestra, Chorus, and soloists performed the Gloria section of the *Mass in B Minor* and the Christmas section of the *Messiah*. From the first row in the balcony, Cyndi and I listened to the finest sounds of the human spirit. Those soaring harmonies and polyphonies are two of the great galley oars of human consciousness, rowing us across the galaxies.

Doc, the marine biologist and sole proprietor of Western Biological Laboratories in John Steinbeck's novel, Cannery Row, plays recordings of Gregorian chants of the Sistine Choir in his lab at high volume. He hears the planet's "music of the spheres" in the flow of Pacific tide pools and in Vatican chants. And, according to Paul Winter, in the liner notes to his 1978 album *Common Ground*, whales, wolves, and eagles all perform their music in the same key—D-flat. But a musical consort is one thing. A whale is another. Humans have, as Wallace Stevens writes, "a maker's rage to order," to order—

> . . . words of the sea,
> Words of the fragrant portals, dimly-starred,
> And of ourselves and of our origins,
> In ghostlier demarcations, keener sounds.

The sound of the singer in that poem, "the single artificer of the world," is—

> More even than her voice, and ours, among
> The meaningless plungings of water and the wind,
> Theatrical distances, bronze shadows heaped
> On high horizons, mountainous atmospheres
> Of sky and sea.

Here I am, writing in words what is beyond words—gestalt glimpses of "the whole that is other than the sum of the parts."

SEA WASHES SAND SCOURS SEA
(for Maria's wedding, 1993)

> *No hay camino. Se hace el camino al andar.*
> —Antonio Machado

Walking the shore that day, each reaches down
for stones from time to time, the other talking,
her eye finding stones like purple berries,
his hand holding a cloud-light shell to her.

Seas they cannot yet see are ancient seas;
trees they will later pass are not yet trees.
Shore that he looks back to turns to haze,
and sand that she imagines turns to shore.

He says, "Sea washes sand scours sea."
"And sand drinks sea drowns sand," says she.
Voices of gulls call through them on the wind;
the dog circles out beyond their voices.

"All that proceeds recedes," he says at last.
"That you and I are here," she says, "is all."
The man watches the woman watches the man.
The woman loves the man loves the woman.

The day does not diminish other days;
they gain a newer language from the day.
Though wave by step their footprints wash away,
The day does not diminish other days.

-][-

Armand Dembski

The Dead Are Sunning Themselves

In the cemetery across the street
the dead are sunning themselves.
In the heat their stones shift and lean,
lounge chairs on a ship's green deck,
graveside flags flying, flowers
under sail on a beautiful day
to be dead, to squint in the fleck
and glitter of quartz, in the glare
of monument white,
the years washed smooth and blind,
the names grown foreign
on an immigrant manifest.

April was cold, but today
even the dead see possibilities.
They move their stiffened joints, stretch,
crack their backs, watch for the mail,
ask: "Is there someplace I have to be
today? What day is this? Saturday?
Sunday? I can't remember what day
it is anymore. Is there anything
to eat? Nothing to drink?

This planet swells with fuel!
Hear the pulse of the axis, the turn
of the driveshaft, the groan below
the waterline. Feel the deep churn
of May under the warming sod.

Cyndi Vander Ven

Meanwhile You and I Say We

The blue spruce swallows a cardinal then
the sun passes a car on the expressway far
and goes down just goes down undeclared.
January. Meanwhile you and I say we
will not be dimmed by winter. Our eyes
will not lose sight. We will sing and our hearts' valves
will wink in time. How love will alter law to move
earth's axis we don't know. Or how such meddling
will muddy seasons we just cannot imagine.
How we will keep the light shining in us
across the cold plain under the cliff of our dying
puzzles me but know how my hand
finds yours in the vast dark of the bed.
How your breathing fills my lungs.
How your blood washes my cells.
How your mouth speaks these syllables into sense.

Cyndi Vander Ven

WAITING FOR THE TRAIN TO STOP

We take the train together, or,
I might say, we each ride the train
of the other, part of us waiting
for the train to stop,
for that unbreathing moment
when the conductor motions
to one or the other.

What we want is a long ride
together, through neighborhoods,
canyons, past flower fields,
beside white waves where
the rails curl near the shore,
till at last satisfied
we come, side by side,
to a slow stop,
gathered, ceremonial, laughing
at some misspoken compliment,
retelling a nearly forgotten
poignance, stepping down
together at the station.
Here we are at last,
done, you and I,
oh love, old friend.

Now imagine worse,
the sudden lurch
somewhere across the plains,
when the brakes lock,
the sparks scatter
in the burning air,
each of us reaches

for the other, but one
of us has gone, not back
into the dull sky of the East,
nor down into the hard
earth of the West, but gone,
somehow, into too much, too little,
for an idea or a metaphor.

-][-

Cyndi Vander Ven

In Spurano di Ossuccio

I carry it around in my head
as if my brain had pockets
like a winter coat,
the one with the inside pocket
to the left of the zipper,
where a novel would sew it
over my heart, a pocket
I don't find for two years
till one day I want a safe slot
for the letter I think I might mail someday,
the words rewriting my life,
traveling up and down the snowbound
Wildwood driveway, crinkling
for the first month or so, till
it finally wears soft.
I take it out sometimes, reading
your name and the note: Open
when I die.

The letter might be an apology
for being late, for a neglected errand,
or, like a soldier's letter home,
a plea for you to wait somewhere
in a green park, a promise to come
to you in some meadow beyond.
Or a bare remembrance:
the window in the bedroom
in Spurano di Ossuccio, open,
wide and screenless, aromas
of night pour over the sill
to pool beside you where you dream,
in islands of canaries and on
the palmy beach at Juan Dolio.

Cyndi Vander Ven

WE WILL ALWAYS BE THERE

Remember when Fred and Ginger danced in our shadow that year in Cairo? It was during the war, or was it later at Callanwolde, when Gabriella asked us not to salsa? Or it may have been on the patio of the Albatross in the Dominican. We should have danced on the rooftop in Astros at night, with wind blowing off the Argonic Gulf, and orange lights washing the walls of the castle above Paralio, where the old men slept in their apartments above the little stores, and the calico cat dozed next to the white ducks beside the old fishing boat.

We will always be there. We will always walk the path to the top of Akrokorinthos, following the ragged man who stirred the hot air with his fluttering hands and disappeared into the empty tower.

We will always walk along Via del Pellegrino and Via Monserrato and Via Santa Maria in Monticelli, all paths to the Campo where the blue-eyed travelers sit at the tables of La Carbonara, watching the dogs drink from the faucets of Rome, where the children ride their bicycles around the other lovers who lay their wreaths at the feet of the burned martyr, Giordano.

We will always be there, having dinner at Santa Cristina off the Via Nazionale, talking with Enrico and Morena, drinking prosecco, and, before the radicchio and gruyere salad, bowing.

MIXEL 1.0: ITS BEGINNING AND END IN [*ENTER GHOST*]

Collage has . . . been thought of as 'the manifestation of a specific historical moment, a moment of crisis in consciousness,' both social and political. This specific historical moment can be called modernity, and is directly related to capitalism and reproduction. (Bell/Frascina)

When Tom asked me if I would like to illustrate [*Enter Ghost*] using the iPad Mixel app, I immediately thought of the larger Mixel community and what it could mean to collaborate on an art project. The heart of Mixel was, after all, collaboration: someone created a digital collage and one by one, friends took the original and remixed it into unique new pieces. At times there were over a hundred remixes of these archetypes. Collaboration in extremis. Invitations were extended, and the art you see in [*Enter Ghost*] is the result. It became a bittersweet endeavor, however, because less than a year after its creation, and a few months into the [*Enter Ghost*] project, the creators of Mixel announced that they were dismantling it.

When I joined Mixel, I had no interest in the social aspect of the app; I just wanted to play at art. Soon, however, I began "liking" posted work. People began making comments on my work, then "following" me. I followed others, making comments as to their creativity, evocative nature, or humor. Comments developed into relationships through these non-linear conversations. I developed friends atcompass extremes: the expanse of Europe and impossible pockets of the Middle East; Asia—Japan, China, India, as well as small, lesser-known archipelagos; from the southern tip of South America to the northern climes of Russia. Most of the United States. The Mixel community grew as the depth and breadth of the base expanded. The ever-evolving, productive core stayed in regular touch, and from that came thousands of offshoots similar to a family tree. The closer you were to that core, like siblings or cousins on the tree, the more like family you became. The beauty of it was that anyone from around the world could graft themselves as closely into the heart of the community as they wished to be. When my hand was in a cast, I posted a picture of it and invited people to sign it; what came back were dozens of comic scenes with my hand in cast as the central character and all with get well wishes. And when another of our Mixelers found she was losing her eyesight and wouldn't be able to create with our group any longer, Mixel arranged a call-in where anyone from around the world who wished could call and leave a message for her. That recording was then posted privately, given to her and the rest of us. It was the first time that we "heard" each other's voices—care and concern given in a beautiful array of accents; she wasn't the only emotional one.

Collage as an art medium has been around since at least the second century BCE in China. More popularly, Picasso and Braque brought it into twentieth century art with wallpaper, oilcloth, rope, and other found objects (Bell). With the advent of computers and software such as the Adobe products and various paint programs, digital montages of photographs proliferated, but not until Mixel was there a platform that allowed for the possibility of two things: 1) non-artists to produce some pretty good art with the tools Mixel provided, and 2) many of those people to form not just the hit-and-miss relationships that most social media apps produce, but real, lasting, supportive bonds.

Much of what we are about today as creators and consumers is shortsighted. Television shows, radio DJs, performance art, digital code, software, clothing fads, apps, special effects, sound bites—an information overload—comes packaged to or by us so neatly, so wonderfully, and then is so readily torn from us to be replaced by the next and greatest, or the expectations of us are so great that we become numbed to inaction or flattened by deadlines. We maneuver life as through the Fields of Asphodel.

Mixel 1.0 broke through that mundanity, reaching a level of humanity in a social community not usually experienced in the digital world. Mixel, the brainchild of Khoi Vinh, former *New York Times* digital design director, and MIT computer science phenom Scott Ostler, was launched in November 2011 (Kafka). Initially Vinh said, "We don't want art to be something monumental that makes people feel intimidated. Rather, we want to take people that would never really engage with art apps and turn them into engaged, passionate visual communicators" (Konstine).

In the end, Vinh blamed the app: it was intimidating. He blamed the community: what we were turning out intimidated new and prospective Mixelers. We didn't attract enough new users. And, "The problem, Vinh wrote, was that 'the Mixel community is not as large as it would have to be in order for us to sustain it as a business.' Vinh explained to *Macworld* that, 'Like a lot of social networks, we were going for scale, so we really wanted to hit a critical mass—millions, even many millions, of users—and we didn't really get there.'" (Friedman). Our community was devastated. Vinh, Ostler, and their investors turned their attention to a new app—Mixel 2.0 for iPhone only—merely a vehicle to take the photos on your phone and place them in pre-made slots like a picture frame. It was not an art program, and in the end it wasn't going to sustain a social community either.

What happened to Vinh's desire for "engaged, passionate visual communicators?" It was subsumed under the rubric of shortsighted corporate dogma. Our Mixel base pleaded as a group that they not close down Mixel 1.0, but there was no going back; their direction had been altered months before they announced their decision to us and mere months after their initial launch. Their base could've been their strength. We would've bent over backwards for them, raised money, bought their product where it had been free, worked on raising awareness—if only we knew they were in need. We supported each other; we would've supported our company. This is the story, in miniature, of so much of what needs to change within us, within America—this short-sightedness when it comes to others. But the Mixel *community* gives me hope of possibility. Some of us from around the world still meet and create art elsewhere on the web.

Cyndi Vander Ven
December 2012

Bell, Emily. "Collage." *The University of Chicago: Theories of Media: Keywords Glossary: Collage*. Web. Winter 2007.

"Collage." *Wikipedia: The Free Encyclopedia.* The Wikipedia Foundation, Inc. 22 July 2004. Web. 15 January 2013.

Constine, Josh. "Become an Artist with Mixel's Remixable iPad Collage App." *TechCrunch.* Web. 9 November 2011.

Friedman, Lex. "Collage App Mixel Will Shut Down in September." *Macworld.* Web. 9 August 2012.

Frascina, Francis. "Collage: Conceptual and Historical Overview." In *Encyclopedia of Aesthetics*: 382-382. New York: Oxford University Press, 1998.

Kafka, Peter. "Mixel, Take Two: After a High Profile App Fails, its Founders Try Again (Q & A)." Media. *All Things D.* Web. 29 August 2012.

The Artists

Ed Brandt graduated with a BA in Painting from Lewis University in Romeoville, Illinois. It was there he discovered his passion for creativity and technology and how the two work hand-in-hand in personal expression. For over seventeen years Ed has worked professionally as a graphic designer, helping brand, market, and promote businesses and products, both large and small. When he is not in the office he can be found processing other creative ideas; whether in front of a canvas, behind the lens of a camera, or experimenting with another creative medium, art has always played a major role in his life.

Jay Cagle is a software development manager living in Cincinnati, Ohio. He enjoys traveling and photography and loved Mixel as a medium for creative expression. His photography can be viewed at www.flickr.com/photos/cajaygle.

Nantanat Choisutcharit (nicknamed Puilui or Pui) was born and raised in Bangkok, Thailand, but now lives in Grass Valley, California, where she manages a Thai restaurant. She studied Ceramics and Applied Art at Rangsit University. Pui loves food, traveling, and creating art.

Heidi Cobb was born in Karlsruhe, Germany. She met and married an American soldier boy, leaving Germany for the U.S. in the early eighties. She is the mother of two adult children and one very special grandchild. Being the fifth of seven children and growing up without any luxury at all, she never got the chance to develop any creative gifts she may have had, nor was exposed to the arts in any form. She just knew that she admired paintings, museums, antiques, music—anything that required creativity. Photography is where her heart is now; several years ago she picked up a camera and began to take photos, amazed at what a picture can reveal, how it conveys the world around us and the people in it. Since that day she has been hooked. She and her husband moved back to Germany temporarily in October 2012, and plan on returning to Virginia in 2014—a date she anxiously anticipates.

John S. DeFord retired from a career in human service in 2006. He has been a lifelong amateur artist working in a variety of media. A progressive neurological disorder caused him to turn to digital media for creative expression. He now works exclusively in photography and in other digital arts similar to Mixel. He lives in Bad Axe, Michigan. You can see more of his art at john-deford.blogspot.com.

Armand Dembski is forty-one years old and along with his family he is the property manager of a picturesque estate that is within sight of Mont Sainte-Victoire in Provence, France—a mountain painted by Paul Cézanne many times. He loves art in many forms: painting, photography, design, and enjoyed discovering and sharing art through the Mixel medium.

Samira Emelie started as a writer, moved crowds as a DJ for twelve years, and recently delved into digital art. She will always be a poet, no matter the medium. Her workdays consist of sketching prototypes and writing code as an information architect. She currently resides in Oakland, California. Visit samiraemelie.deviantart.com to see more of her artwork.

Akira Hashiguchi has been in beauty salon management for twenty years in Sendai, Japan. He has been painting and photographing local events for many years, and had an exhibition of his art and photos published. In recent years he has been actively producing video works through YouTube. He looks forward to interacting with other overseas creators of art, beauty, and fashion through iPad. See some of his videos at www.youtube.com/user/godbeam.

Sandy Brown Jensen is a digital storyteller, photographer, poet and bon vivant from Eugene, Oregon. She teaches writing and is a faculty technology specialist at Lane Community College. Her work can be viewed at pln.lanecc.net/mindonfire.

Robert "Monte" Merritt is an attorney in private practice in the field of consumer protection law and regulation, and related practical issues. From 1995 to 2005 Mr. Merritt was in-house counsel, and SVP and Associate General Counsel, to Providian Financial Corporation. From 1991 to 1995 Mr. Merritt was a litigation associate in the San Francisco office of Heller, Ehrman.

In recent years Mr. Merritt has been devoting most of his time and attention to a software startup in the information curation and personal productivity space founded with his brother Mark. He believes that Mixel, before its commercial failure, was a creative outlet for personal expression in a networked community setting, and was rapidly iterating itself through collaborative creation, sharing, and recombination of ideas. Criticism and appreciation were merging into the art itself (or quasi-art, as some would have it). Mr. Merritt lives in Oakland, California, with his wife of twenty years, Audrey, and sixteen-year-old daughter, Annie. Mr. Merritt has to thank his older daughter, Isabel (Izzy), for getting him involved pretty early in Mixel.

Sandrine Menorah Nzenza was born in Belgium of African parents. She holds a university degree in Germanic languages and literature with her thesis on the duality of people living between two cultures: "Het Reismotief en de zoektocht naar identiteit in het werk van Marion Bloem." Sandrine translated "The Dead are Sunning Themselves" and "A Work of the Heart's Trying" from English into French to provide better grounding for Armand Dembski's Mixel art. She currently resides in Dublin, Ireland.

Cyndi Vander Ven holds an MFA in Creative Writing from the University of Notre Dame where she also fed some fiction and poetry back into the system via the MFA program's magazine, *The Bend*. She created the cover art for *A Campus Becoming*, the 2011 Wolfson Press book by Tom Vander Ven and Patrick Furlong. Before retiring early to spend time traveling with her husband, her career spanned a variety of fields: business administration; entrepreneurship; pharmaceutical sales; and teaching literature, writing, and writing about literature. She has dabbled in digital art since the Adobe products' inception, creating everything from T-shirt art to, well, book cover design. She currently resides in Atlanta, Georgia.

Napin Viriyasathien, as an exchange student from Bankok, Thailand, attended Lakeview Academy in Gainsville, Georgia, for her senior year of high school. After graduation, she returned to Thailand to study chemical engineering at Sirindhorn International Institute of Technology, Thammasat University. She hopes to study management or economics for her master's degree and would like to become a chemical engineer at an international company. Pin translated "Fall of the Monarch" into Thai for Nantanat Choisutcharit so she could better get a feel for the Mixel she wanted to create.

-][-